SUGAR CREEK GANG
20
The BULL FIGHTER

Paul Hutchens

MOODY PRESS
CHICAGO

Original Title: *10,000 Minutes at Sugar Creek*

ISBN: 0-8024-7024-6

1 3 5 7 9 10 8 6 4 2

Printed in the United States of America

PREFACE

Hi—from a member of the Sugar Creek Gang!

It's just that I don't know which one I am. When I was good, I was Little Jim. When I did bad things—well, sometimes I was Bill Collins or even mischievous Poetry.

You see, I am the daughter of Paul Hutchens, and I·spent many an hour listening to him read his manuscript as far as he had written it that particular day. I went along to the north woods of Minnesota, to Colorado, and to the various other places he would go to find something different for the Gang to do.

Now the years have passed—more than fifty, actually. My father is in heaven, but the Gang goes on. All thirty-six books are still in print and now are being updated for today's readers with input from my five children, who also span the decades from the '50s to the '70s.

The real Sugar Creek is in Indiana, and my father and his six brothers were the original Gang. But the idea of the books and their ministry were and are the Lord's. It is He who keeps the Gang going.

PAULINE HUTCHENS WILSON

1

The very thought of my city cousin coming to visit us for a whole week while his parents went on a vacation was enough to start a whirlwind in my mind.

A whirlwind, you know, is a baby-sized rotating windstorm. On most any ordinary summer day around our farm, you can expect to see one of these friendly fun makers spiraling out across the fields or through the woods like a little funnel of wind. It laughs along, carrying with it a lot of different things such as dry leaves and grass and feathers from our chicken yard or dust from the path that goes from the iron pitcher pump across the barnyard to the barn, or anything else that's loose and light.

Away the little whirlwind goes, *whirlety-sizzle*, like an excited boy running in circles. Is it ever fun to toss yourself into one of them and go racing along with it and in it. Nearly every time I get into the middle of one, though, it acts as if it can't stand having a red-haired boy getting mixed up in it, and all of a sudden it isn't a whirlwind anymore. All the leaves and grass and dust and stuff stop whirling and just sail around in the sky awhile before they come floating down all over the place.

So Wally, my whirlwind city cousin, was coming to visit us. He not only had a lot of mis-chievous ideas in his mind, but he didn't like to be told anything, such as how to do a thing and especially *not* to do a thing.

The worst thing was, he was going to bring with him his copper-colored dog, which he had named Alexander the Coppersmith and which didn't have any good country manners. Certainly there would be plenty of excitement around the place, and some of it would be dangerous. Just how dangerous, I couldn't tell until Wally and his dog got there.

There isn't any boy who likes excitement more than I do, and I even like it a little bit dangerous, as well as mysterious, but I *didn't* want Wally to come, and I *didn't* want Alexander the Coppersmith either.

Honest to goodness, I never heard or saw or smelled such a frisky, uncontrollable, uned-ucated, ill-mannered dog without any good country breeding, from his mischievous muz-zle all the way back to his "feather."

Maybe you didn't know that dogs have feathers, but they do. "Feather" is the name of the tip end of a dog's tail. It's the featherlike hair that grows on the very, very end. I didn't know that myself until I read it in a book about dogs, which Dad gave me for my birthday.

When I had first seen Wally's dog, I thought it was an Airedale. Wally was extraproud of his copper-colored quadruped because he could do several things, such as sit up and bark when he wanted food.

I never will forget what happened the year Wally brought him the first time. It was on a Thanksgiving Day. Wally had been so sure that if we tied our turkey's neck to a rope and tied the other end of the rope to Alexander that he would lead the turkey all around the pen like a boy leading a pony. We tried it, and for a while it was a lot of fun watching the dog do his stuff. The turkey followed along behind like a baby chicken following its mother, until all of a sudden our old black and white cat, Mixy, came arching her back and rubbing her sides against things the way cats do. A second later, Alexander was making a wild dog dash toward Mixy. At that very second also, Mixy made a wild cat dash out across our barnyard toward the barn.

Alexander forgot his neck was tied to a turkey's neck. He dragged the turkey *flip-floppety-sizzle* behind him.

You can believe that I, Bill Collins, came to the quickest life I had ever come to. I started to make a wild dash for the gate of the turkey pen to shut it so that Alexander couldn't get out to catch Mixy, and also so the turkey couldn't get out, because it was the very turkey we had been saving for months to have for Thanksgiving dinner.

Besides, Mixy was my very favorite cat friend, and I couldn't stand the thought of her getting hurt, although I knew she was a fierce fighter and could probably take care of herself if the dog did catch up with her. I had seen her lick the daylights out of several of our neighborhood dogs. Boy oh boy, when she gets her temper up, she can lick the stuffings out of the fightingest dog in the whole territory.

Squash! Wham! *Floppety-gobblety-sizzle!* Even though Mixy got to the barn safely, and Wally finally got Alexander the Coppersmith quieted down, the turkey's neck was broken, so Dad had to come and finish killing it, which he did, thirty minutes sooner than he would have anyway.

Even though Wally had been training his dog the best he could, that dog didn't seem to have any control of his emotions whenever there was a cat around.

And now Wally was coming again, and it was *that* dog he was bringing with him! Dad and I were talking it over one day about a month before Wally and Alexander arrived.

"Don't worry," my reddish brown mustached, bushy eyebrowed father said. "He will be a year older and a year smarter than he was last year." Except that Dad was thinking about Wally.

"He'll be a year older and a year dumber," I said, thinking about the dog.

"You can't say things like that about one of your relatives."

"I mean the dog will be a year dumber."

"And besides," Dad said, "Wally is not only your cousin. He is your Aunt Belle's only son, and an only son is sometimes a problem."

"I am your only son, too, and I hope I am not as wild as he is."

"I hope so myself," Dad said.

For a second I was half mad.

But Wally was really bad. He just couldn't learn anything. He couldn't be *told* anything, and he was always wanting to do what he wanted to do, whether anyone else wanted him to do it or wanted to do it with him. And it wasn't because he had red hair and freckles, because I had them, and I certainly wasn't that independent a person—not all the time. Not even half the time.

Dad tried to make me look at things more cheerfully by saying, "The Lord hasn't finished making Wally yet. He's only been working on him ten years, and about the only tools He has had to work with are his parents. Parents have a lot to do with what a boy turns out to be."

Because Dad and I were always joking with each other, I asked, "Is that why I'm such a good boy—I have such good parents?"

Dad grinned under his mustache and with his eyes and said, "You *are* a pretty good boy—don't you think?"

"I hate to say it," I said.

I remembered that when I was just a little guy, Dad would scoop me up in his arms and hug me. But that would look silly for a red-haired, freckle-faced boy as old as I was to be getting picked up by his father at nine o'clock in the morning. Besides, Dad had that bristly mustache, and what boy in his right mind would want to get mixed up with that? It'd be as bad as a dog getting mixed up with a fat porcupine.

Just thinking that reminded me of Wally

once more and also of his uncontrollable dog, and I was worried again. Nothing Dad could say that morning helped a bit. I simply couldn't get reconciled to the idea of losing a whole week of my life.

Mom had her say-so on the subject that same day. "I'll expect you to put on your very best manners when your Aunt Belle and Uncle Amos are here—for a very special reason."

"Why?" I said. "What reason?"

Mom was taking an apple pie out of the oven at the time, and I was smelling pie and thinking maybe it might not be such a bad thing to have Wally come. Every time we had company at our house, she always baked a lot of pies and cookies and stuff.

"Don't you know?" she asked.

"I don't see any special reason why I have to be extragood when such an extrabad boy is coming to see me," I said.

She answered, "Ask your father, then," which a little later I did when my dad and I were out in the garden hoeing potatoes.

"How come I have to be an extragood boy when Wally is here? How can I be, when it is hard enough just being as good as I am?"

"Can't you guess?" he asked.

I racked my brain to try to think what he was thinking of—and couldn't and said so.

"Well, let it go at that. You'll probably think of it yourself."

Mom called from the back door then, saying, "Telephone, Bill!"

I dropped my potato hoe as if it were a hot potato and started on the run, not knowing who wanted to talk to me but hoping it would be one of the gang, hoping especially it would be Poetry, the gang's barrel-shaped member.

And sure enough it was. He was coming over to my house right after lunch. "Have I ever got a surprise for you!" he said in his usual squawky voice.

Boy oh boy, did it ever feel good when Poetry talked like that. He had a detective mind and also what is called an "inventive" mind. He was always thinking up something new for us to do, and nearly always it was something especially interesting or exciting. Sometimes it was dangerous, but it was always fun!

A little later, when he hung up, I was tingling all over. My almost best friend, Poetry, was coming to play with me that afternoon, and he had a surprise. It could be—well, almost anything!

Right after the noon meal, he came sauntering over to our place. He stopped and waited for me in the big rope swing under the walnut tree beside the road. I was just about to take my last bite of blackberry pie when I looked out the east screen door and saw him. I also heard him making one of his fancy bird-calls, which was half like a harp and half like a musical whistle. It seemed to say, "Bill Collins! Bill Collins! Skip the dishes!"—which I knew I shouldn't do, and didn't.

Dad also heard Poetry's whistle, and his

voice came out from under his mustache, say-ing, "You boys have plans for the afternoon?" The way he said it was like a cowboy's lasso set-tling down over a calf's neck. I felt myself and my plan for the afternoon being stopped in their tracks.

"We *did* have," I said. "Is there something I ought to do around the house and garden first?"

"First and second and third," he answered. "The dishes first, the potato patch second, and the barn third." He stopped, and I thought I saw him wink at Mom.

Not being sure, I used a very cheerful voice, saying, "OK, I'll hurry out and tell Poetry to go on home. We were only going on a hike anyway."

"And maybe go swimming also?" Dad's voice said again.

"I'll go out right now and tell him he shouldn't have come." In a flash I was off the bench I had been sitting on. I was halfway through the screen door before Dad tightened the noose of his lasso with "STOP!" in a thun-dery voice.

I stopped stock-still, then stumbled down the steps and stopped again in a tangled-up heap as the door I'd gone through slammed shut.

It was quite a while later before Poetry and I got started on our hike—he having helped me with the different kinds of work I had to do first.

"You're a good boy," Mom said to Poetry as he and I were getting a drink at the iron pitcher pump just before leaving.

"Am I?" Poetry asked politely. Then he added, "Will you tell my mother that sometime?"

"She knows it. She told me that herself once." Mom was wearing her very friendly mother face, the kind that was especially nice when we had company at our house.

"Maybe *your* mother could tell my mother to tell *me* that, too," I suggested to Poetry.

Mom laughed a friendly laugh. "Oh, Bill Collins, you *know* you are a good boy."

"You know it, and I know it," I said, "but you might tell my *father* that sometime."

I pumped another cup of cold water and tossed it over the horse trough, where it surprised a dozen yellow butterflies that had gathered around a little pool of water. The butterflies shot up into the air in different directions like sparks from a log fire do when you poke a stick into it, or as if a whirlwind had come along and swooped them all up into the air. Then they settled down again around the water pool.

Well, Poetry and I were finally off *lickety-sizzle* across the yard, past "Theodore Collins" on the tin mailbox, across the dusty gravel road, over the rail fence—I vaulting over and Poetry hoisting his roly-poly body over the top rail—and the two of us racing barefoot in the path that had been made by boys running toward the spring.

On the way, I was hoping that some of the rest of the gang would be there, such as spindle-legged Dragonfly, the pop-eyed member whose nose turns south at the end, or Little Jim, with his mouselike face and curly hair—the only one of the gang who could play the piano and also maybe the only one of us for sure about whom, if his mother told him he was a good boy, it would be the truth any time of day she happened to say it.

2

Even as Poetry and I ran through the woods, I was thinking and wondering how I would ever live through Wally and Alexander the Coppersmith's visit. But there wasn't a thing I could do to stop their coming. I would just have to endure it.

I was remembering that other time Wally had spent a whole, never-to-be-forgotten, awful day and night at our house. Alexander had about six bad habits. One was, he would make a wild dash for every car that came down the Sugar Creek road and would bark at it and run alongside its front wheel, acting as if he hated the very sight of a moving car. Sometimes he would follow it clear down to the north road—or at least until it outran him and he was so far behind he gave up. Then he would come trotting, panting, and grinning dog style back to "Theodore Collins" on our mailbox and wag his tail as much to say, "Boy oh boy, did I ever chase that car down the road! I never saw a car yet I couldn't chase away." Only maybe, instead of saying, "Boy oh boy," he was saying, "Dog oh dog."

Then, even before he got through bragging on himself for scaring a car out of the neighborhood, he would spy Mixy or one of our old hens or roosters and would be off again.

Another bad habit was to bark at night when everyone wanted to sleep. He slept—or was supposed to sleep—on a rug in the little tent we had put up for him under the grape arbor, but it seemed he was the most wide awake dog that was ever born. He would start barking at something he saw or heard, or thought he saw or heard, and keep it up until he'd wake up everybody in the house—except Wally, who was the soundest sleeper I ever saw or heard.

Wally sounded like a saw going through a hickory log, and he and Alexander the Coppersmith together were like a big bass viol solo with a barking dog accompaniment.

Alexander also had two or three other bad habits, but the worst one—the one that would get him into the worst trouble before our topsy-turvy week was over—was that he wasn't scared of anything. Everything he saw or smelled started him into action, and he would make a running dive for it, teeth first—cat, chicken, duck, goose, rabbit, squirrel, anything.

I told Poetry all about how Wally the Whirlwind and Alexander the Coppersmith, the scatterbrained dog, were coming to spend a whole terrible week at our house. And how they would be all over the whole place and all around Sugar Creek and up and down and in it, upsetting the peace of its quiet shores. And how the gang might have to take Wally in and let him and his dog go on hikes with us and go swimming and do things!

But Poetry tried to console me by saying in his squawky voice, "I was dumb myself once, and look at me now."

It seemed there never was a time when Poetry wasn't mischievous. About the only time he had a sober face was when we were in church and our minister was praying or preaching. Our minister was the father of Sylvia, the extranice girl whom Big Jim, the leader of our gang, thought was extranice—nicer than anybody else in the whole world.

Well, when Poetry said, "I used to be dumb myself," I looked at his roly-poly back—he was trotting along in front of me at the time—and at his big bare feet and his turned-up overalls. I answered him, "You're still kind of *thick*."

"That's not funny." Away he went on a faster running wobble, with me right after him, toward the Sugar Creek bridge.

When we came to the north road, we scrambled over the rail fence and stopped awhile on the bridge itself. Then we lay down on our stomachs on the bridge's board floor. We looked over the edge into the deep, clear, quiet water, where there were scores and scores of big suckers lazily lying down there, all of them headed upstream.

Those fish certainly were taking life easy. Many a time we had tried tempting them with nice fishing worms, but they were not interested.

All they seemed to want to do was to lie around and sleep.

We tossed in a few stones to scare the suckers, but they didn't stay scared very long. They were like a boy being waked up too early in the morning. Pretty soon they were settled down again and acting lazier than ever, taking their afternoon nap.

"They never have to do any dishes or hoe any potatoes," I said.

"Or eat any blackberry pie," Poetry said. "The poor fish!"

Then we stood up, shook the iron girders of the bridge a few times just to hear them rattle, and went on toward where we had been going in the first place, which was down to the old trash dump on the other side of the mouth of the branch.

Nearly every weekend, people would drive along the dusty lane that skirted the brow of the hill just above Sugar Creek. They would stop then and throw out trash that had accumulated around their houses, such as old bottles, tin cans, typewriter ribbon boxes, and pieces of plumbing and stuff. Sometimes there would be something very pretty or different, which members of the gang could add to their collection.

Well, it was a lucky day for us. We found a lot of extra-interesting things, and it looked as if we were the first boys in the neighborhood to sort them over. In a little while I had quite a pile of stuff I wanted, including a purple perfume bottle that was shaped like a tiger and an alarm clock that, when I shook it and accidentally dropped it, started to run. The alarm also worked.

"Maybe all it needed was a good shaking up."

"You'd run too if somebody shook you that hard," Poetry said. "But you better not let your folks know you have it, or you'll be getting up too early in the morning from now on."

"I won't need one next month," I said. "I won't even get to go to sleep with Alexander the Coppersmith here. That dog'll bark all night, and Wally'll snore all night."

A little later Poetry was looking around near the water when he let out an astonished yell. "Of all the ignorant people! Somebody has thrown away a lot of books!"

Well, if there was anything I liked better than anything else, it was a good book. Both my parents were always reading, and I had sort of caught the reading habit from them, the way a boy catches the measles or mumps from another boy.

In seconds I was half sliding and half climbing down to where Poetry was picking up one book after another and stacking them on a rocky ledge beside him.

But when I saw what kind of books they were, I said, "Aw, they are just some old schoolbooks. No wonder they threw them away."

And that's what most of them were—a spelling book that was half worn out, with a lot of pages missing; an atlas of the world that was dated fifty years ago; and different kinds of old-fashioned textbooks. "Just leave them," I said. "They aren't worth carrying home."

"But, look!" Poetry cried excitedly. "Here is a book of poems!" He opened the book, and before I could have stopped him, if I had wanted to, he had started to read one.

> "I had a little pussy,
> Its coat was silver gray;
> It lived down in the meadow,
> It never ran away.
> It always was a pussy,
> It'll never be a cat,
> Because it was a pussy willow—
> Now what do you think of that?"

It wasn't a bad poem. In fact, it was kind of cute, I thought, and decided Poetry could keep that book anyway, since he liked poetry so much.

If there was anything I liked better than anything else growing around Sugar Creek, it was a pussy willow, which is a shrub that grows along the bayou and in other places where the soil is wet. It is one of the first signs to tell you that winter is dying and that spring has honest to goodness been born. When you see a pussy willow with its reddish brown bark all decorated with silky, silvery tufts of hair, even before its bright green leaves come out, you get a wonderful feeling. It makes a boy feel good just to *think* about a Sugar Creek pussy willow.

Then I thought of Wally's coming and of his dog, and that made me feel like throwing things. So I started picking up stones and tossing them into the fast-flowing creek.

Poetry caught my half-mad mood and quickly started tossing in stones, too. A minute later, rocks were *really* flying.

It felt good to let off steam that way. I was still throwing things when Poetry picked up a big corrugated box and decided to make a boat.

The box did look like a square boat dancing on the waves. And the water acted as if it was happy to get something that would float. It whirled the carton around and carried it toward the island, where the current was strongest, and there it caught in the crotch of an overhanging willow and stopped. We decided to use the box for a target, and right away all kinds of stones were flying thick and fast toward it, most of them landing in the carton.

While I was still working off my temper, I spotted another book, and the very second I saw its title, I wanted it. It was *All Kinds of Dogs and How to Train Them.* A picture on the book's jacket was of a laughing, friendly faced collie.

I made a grab for the book, but Poetry beat me to it. Before I could stop him, he had tossed the *book* into the box, where it landed with a *ker-plop.*

That, I thought, was one book I really wanted. If I was going to have to live a whole week with an uneducated city dog, I at least ought to know something about how an educated dog ought to behave itself.

So, before Mom or Dad could have stopped me if either one of them had been there, I rolled up my overall pant legs to my knees and stepped into the narrow, fast-running, singing riffle, wading as fast as I could toward the Sugar Creek island where the box with the book in it was lodged against the overhanging willow.

I figured that the box boat would soon sink with all the weight of the stones we had thrown into it. So I hurried as fast as a boy can who has orders from his parents not to get his new overalls wet. The water was knee-deep, and the stones and stuff on the bottom made it hard to keep my balance.

"Hurry up," Poetry yelled to me. "It might sink!"

But how could I? My bare feet kept slipping on round stones and bottles and different things that some dumb boys had thrown into the creek. Soon I would be there, though, and would have the book, if only—

Then Poetry yelled, "Quick! It's breaking away from the willow! It'll be gone downstream in a minute!"

I took a fast worried look and saw that Poetry was right. In seconds, the box boat would be out in the center of the riffle, swirling down the creek, where before long it would get water-soaked and sink, and my book would be both spoiled and lost.

So forgetting my new overalls and my parents' orders not to get them wet, I took several fast steps, took a wild lunge toward the box and the book, stepped on another bottle, lost my balance, and landed *ker-splash* beside the box.

3

There I was, a red-haired, freckle-faced, wet boy, as dumb as Wally's copper-colored dog. I was both happy and unhappy—happy because I had the book and unhappy because of my very wet overalls.

I stood for a minute balancing myself in the riffle. About thirty feet downstream, riding cheerfully along, was our box boat, sailing merrily as if it didn't have a care in the world. Certainly it didn't have to worry about how to explain to its mother how it happened to get all wet.

In my mind's eye I imagined Mom looking me over from red head to bare feet but especially at my overalls, saying, as she nearly always does when she is surprised, "For land's sakes!"

I'd heard her say that once before when I came home all wet, and Dad, who had been there at the time, said, "Not for *land's* sakes, but for the water's sake." Then when I had explained, Dad had said, "I'm afraid that explanation is all wet, too, Bill."

I hurried back across Sugar Creek to the shore and scrambled up the bank to where Poetry was. He had found a tall utility can with a handle on each side, which some lady had thrown away because rust had eaten a little hole in the bottom, and he was filling it with our collection.

We also found a lid for the can, put it on, and pretty soon were up the hill and carrying our treasures down the dusty lane toward his house. One of the first things he said as we plopped along showed that he was a real pal. "We'll stop at our house and get your clothes dried and ironed, and they'll be as good as new."

That made me feel better—so good in fact, especially now that I had the book, that I began to enjoy being alive again.

And that was the way I happened to get started really getting ready for Wally's visit. That book I'd found was packed with the best ideas you ever heard of about how to stop a dog from chasing cars and cats and even how to stop him from barking at night.

Boy oh boy, I thought, as Poetry and I trudged along the lane toward his house. We were swinging the can between us, letting our bare feet go *plop, plop, plop* in the dust and enjoying the feel of the nice warm dirt squishing up between our toes.

I used my left hand to carry my side of the can, and with the other I held the dog book open and read parts of it aloud to Poetry. Poetry carried his side of the can with his right hand and held his book in his left and read different poems to me.

"Listen to this," I said:

"Once a dog has the bad habit of chasing chickens, it is almost impossible to break him of it. The only sure way is to show him a chicken when he is still a pup and let him make friends with it. If your dog has more courage than good sense and rushes blindly into a fight with other dogs, sometimes the best thing for him is to allow him to get a good trouncing by the other, perhaps larger, dog. The only thing is, he may in turn seek satisfaction by attacking dogs smaller than himself so that his sense of importance won't be completely thwarted. A dog likes to feel important."

And Poetry answered,

"When the days get hickey-dickey
And your clothes get sort-o sticky
And you want to pull your shoes off—
Then it's spring!"

"And this," I said, stumbling over a stone in the road and saying, "Ouch!"

"If your dog is a car chaser, have a friend drive past your house and have someone in the car squirt in the dog's face with a water pistol loaded with three parts of water and one part of household ammonia. This will sting, but will not do any permanent harm."

But Poetry hadn't heard a word. The very second I stopped long enough for him to shove in a word or two, he hurried on with another poem, one of the verses being:

"There's a queer uneasy feelin'
   Casts a shedder over me,
And I long to be a-stealin'
   Where the wind blows cool and free;
I'm as restless as a rabbit.
   Nothin' satisfies me quite—
Fer I feel that rovin' habit
   When the fish begin to bite."

"Hey!" I interrupted, suddenly smelling a strong obnoxious odor coming from somewhere.

We both stopped stock-still and smelled.

"It's a skunk!" I exclaimed. "There's a skunk somewhere around here!"

A light breeze was blowing from the direction of an old toolshed in the woods not far from Poetry's dad's barn.

But Poetry didn't seem interested. With his eyes on his book, he only grunted and said, "Oh, didn't you know that? A nice new polecat mother has moved her family from somewhere or other to our toolshed. They live underneath it. But my father says to leave them alone. They won't do any harm unless they get too hungry and feel like they have to eat a few chickens to satisfy their appetites."

"I know that," I said. I also knew that skunks had a very choice diet of grasshoppers and beetles, especially june beetles, or june bugs, and crickets. Grasshoppers are one of the farmer's worst enemies. In the summertime, skunks also eat centipedes and sawflies and locusts and cutworms and sphinx moths and, for variety, a few berries. It is in the winter, when they can't find june bugs and cutworms and grubs, that they get so hungry they sometimes raid a farmer's chicken yard.

"Some of the skunk kids must have gotten into a fight," I said, remembering that a skunk carries a spray gun of his own, filled with a mixture that is a lot stronger than three parts of water and one part of ammonia. He carries it in a musk pouch somewhere on his body, and with it he protects himself from his enemies. He very seldom uses it on members of his own family, unless he gets into a fierce fight or plays too hard and gets too excited or mad or scared.

All of a sudden from beside a wild gooseberry bush, just off to the right of the lane we were walking in, I saw a flash of a boy's faded overalls, a shock of curly hair, and a monkey face. I knew it was Circus—the acrobat of our gang, the one who is the brother of a whole family of nearly all girls.

Also, at that same second, Circus hissed to Poetry and me, saying, "*Sh!* Keep still, you guys. There's a pretty little kitten over there, and I want to catch him for a pet. Don't scare him! I want to sneak up on him and grab him."

I looked in the direction Circus was looking, and what to my wondering eyes should appear but a cute little black and white child skunk. Not knowing we were anywhere around and not being able to smell us because the wind was blowing from his direction to us, he was digging and rooting in the ground beside a fallen log. He was probably looking for a nice grub for his afternoon lunch.

"Look," Circus whispered, "he's dug something up."

The pretty kitty had stopped digging and was chewing away on something. Then, almost right away, he began nosing along the side of the log, stopping every now and then and standing on his haunches the way bears do, listening.

While we were watching, Poetry was reminded of a poem that I had heard him quote before. He started in before Circus could shush him:

"See that little black and white animal
out in the woods?
Say, isn't that little cat pretty?
I went right over to pick it up—
But it wasn't that kind of a kitty!"

In a second Circus was gone, running like a deer toward that innocent-looking skunk, saying just before he left, "I know how to do it without getting shot." He ran toward the fallen log and the wild animal he wanted to catch and make a pet of. Imagine that! Make a pet of a skunk!

As I watched Circus, who usually had very good sense, running pell-mell toward a live polecat that had a very bad scent, it seemed the most ridiculous thing a boy could do. If he should get sprayed with skunk perfume, he would smell like a skunk himself for a week. Of all the idiotic things, anyway!

Circus hadn't galloped more than a few feet before I was imagining what his mother and his six sisters would say when he came home with his clothes all saturated with skunk perfume. Not a one of the rest of the gang's mothers would like the idea either, because we all played with Circus and got into wrestling and tumbling matches with him. And what Sugar Creek Gang mother would want her boy sleeping on a nice clean sheet in her house after he had had a wrestling match with another boy that had a skunk for a pet?

There wasn't time to do any more worrying right then, because things were getting ready to happen. Circus was within ten feet of the little animal before the skunk spied him. Quick as a flash, his bushy black and white tail swished straight up in the air like the beautiful plume on Little Jim's mom's new hat, which she wears on Sunday morning in the Sugar Creek church. At the same time, the kitty started doing a two-legged dance, stamping his front feet as if he was as mad as a hornet.

Boy oh boy, I never saw Circus stop so suddenly and stand so still in my life. He didn't move a muscle for maybe two whole minutes, which seemed like an hour, and that is very hard for a boy to do. Circus and his hoped-for pet now were looking straight at each other the way two strange dogs sometimes do when they meet for the first time and are trying to decide whether to fight or not. Pretty soon one of the dogs decides not to fight, and the other one is glad of it.

I knew from what I had read about skunks that they nearly always swish their tails straight up and dance awhile with their front feet as a warning before they spray you, just as a rattlesnake rattles the rattle on his tail before he strikes.

Circus kept on not moving, and his hoped-for pet kept on keeping his pretty furry tail straight up like a statue of George Washington. He also kept on stamping his front feet as if to say, "One move out of you, Circus Browne, and your name is mud."

After that tense minute was over, the pretty little kitty must have decided Circus wasn't going to hurt him after all. He stopped stamping his feet, he pulled his flag down, and he walked off along the side of the log, going toward Poetry's dad's log cabin toolshed, with Circus trotting along beside him.

It was the most interesting sight and was a good education. *What on earth?* I thought. *What if Alexander the Coppersmith had been here? Alexander would not have used his head at all but, barking, would have made a headfirst dive straight for the black and white animal, only to find that "it wasn't that kind of a kitty."*

"It looks like they are friends already!" Poetry said.

It was unbelievable.

It was still unbelievable a moment later,

when the kitty stopped stock-still and hoisted his flag again. Almost at that same second, Circus went into lightninglike action. He made a quick swooping dive straight for the kitty, grabbed him up by his straight-up bushy tail, and a second later was holding him out at arms' length.

"Come on, you guys!" he yelled to us. "I've got him. He's as harmless as a hornet without a stinger unless his back feet are on the ground."

I happened to know that was the truth from having read it, but I had sort of forgotten.

"Come on! Hurry up! Bring that can, and we'll put him in it!" And Circus started to run straight toward us carrying a handful of black and white dynamite that nobody in his right mind would want to get anywhere near.

At any second, the skunk might wriggle out of Circus's hand. And that would be just too bad, because a skunk can spray at least six times like a six-shooter automatic revolver. And instead of there being a Circus Browne whose name would be mud, there would be Poetry Thompson Mud and William Jasper Collins Mud. And what would Mom say, with my overalls already all wet with Sugar Creek water?

Poetry let out a yell to Circus. "Get away from here with that atomic bomb!" Then he quick hissed to me, "Let's run," which we started to do as fast as we could, carrying our can of treasures up the lane toward Poetry's house, with Circus and his wriggling squirming kitty racing along behind us.

"Stop, you guys!" Circus puffed. "This little rascal will bite me, and I don't dare let him go or he will—*Bill!*" Circus's worried voice almost screamed, not more than twenty feet behind us. "I'll give you half the money I get for him!"

Money, for some reason, didn't look good to me just then. In fact, nothing did. Ordinarily when I am walking or running along that lane, I have the greatest feeling because of the pretty flowers that border it, such as black-eyed Susans with their dark purple centers and long yellow rays that radiate out like the sunflowers in our garden. There are also nearly always violets and ground ivy and sometimes bluebells and asters.

One of the prettiest sights a boy can see is a lot of green grass dotted with white clover, with patches of shade here and there under the maples and elms. It's wonderful to be alive and live most of your life out-of-doors in the fresh air and the Sugar Creek sunshine and be able to go barefoot and feel fine all the time even when you have to work.

But Circus, with a wild animal in one hand, was racing after us, so it was no time to enjoy life. I still had my book on dog education in my right hand, and I noticed Poetry still had his book of poems in his left. All of us were carrying something we didn't want to drop.

I don't know what would have happened if right that second Poetry hadn't stumbled on a tuft of grass in the center of the path. He also caught one of his extralarge big toes in the cuff of his overall leg. Down he went *ker-plop-ker-sizzle* with our can of books and bottles and stuff.

I fell on top of him, the two of us landing in a *bangety-wham* crash and scattering everything in every direction.

Before we could have done anything to stop him, Circus went after our empty can. He quickly grabbed it, plopped his skunk inside, and, putting the lid on tight to be sure his prize didn't get away, sat down on the lid.

"Whew!" he exclaimed.

Poetry and I started to unscramble ourselves and to gather up the things that had been in the can but would never be again. Poetry and I had lost, and Circus had won! While Circus rested, and while his wild animal made a lot of angry noises inside the can, and while for some reason the can didn't have the same smell it had had when we found it, Poetry and I hurried to gather up our treasures. And then we found out we had lost part of our collection.

"Hey!" I said in a disturbed voice. "Where's my alarm clock?" I looked all around and on each side of the lane, behind the wild gooseberry bushes on one side and the chokecherry shrubs on the other. I also looked in the tall grass and among the black-eyed Susans and in the tangle of ground ivy and wild morning glories and still didn't find it.

"You sure you put it in the can?" Poetry asked.

"Of course, I'm sure! That's the most important thing we found—except this book."

"Come and sit here awhile," Circus said, grinning, "and I'll help you look for it."

"Nothing doing!"

Poetry volunteered and started toward Circus, but Circus stopped him. "Oh, no, you don't. You'd squash the can into an accordion."

When I couldn't find my alarm clock anywhere, I began to want it more than anything else, which is how a person feels about something after he has lost it.

And then, unexpectedly, I *heard* it! The alarm was going off! It was the first time in my life I had heard an alarm clock in the middle of a lane in the middle of a woods. Right away it reminded me of home and of five o'clock in the morning, which is the time Dad's alarm clock goes off every day.

But where was the excited jingling sound coming from? For a second my mind was like a whirlwind. I quickly looked around in a fast circle, trying to focus my eyes in the right direction, and I couldn't. For a few seconds, the ringing had a muffled sound as if it was under a pillow, and then it was a lot louder—as though someone had taken the pillow off and put the clock under a dishpan.

Then all of a sudden I knew where it was. "It's inside the can!" I exclaimed. "It's in there with the skunk!"

My eyes met Poetry's, and we both knew what had happened. When we had had our upset, everything had fallen out of the can except the alarm clock, and Circus had plopped his black and white kitty in and clamped on the lid without looking. That kitty, by scrambling and struggling to find a way out, had accidentally set off the alarm.

What excitement!

"I told you skunks were smart," Circus said from his perch on the can in the middle of the lane. "Anybody want to know what time it is?" He quickly stood up and turned around as though he was going to take the lid off.

"Hey," Poetry and I yelled at the same time, "don't you *dare!*" and we dove toward him to stop him. "Keep that lid on!"

"What are you scared of?" Circus asked, his monkey face looking more like a monkey than ever. "There is nothing alarming in this innocent little can."

But that clock must have reminded Circus of what time it really was and of what he ought to do, because he said, "I've got to get going. I'll pay you guys later for your can. How much you want?"

"You pay for my alarm clock too," I said. "Five dollars."

"We'll give you the can, but we want our half of what you get for your kitty," Poetry said. "Don't forget you caught him in our woods!"

With his pocketknife, Circus made a couple of holes in the lid of the can so his kitty wouldn't suffocate. Then, picking up the can in both hands, he started to run toward his house, which is right across the road from Big Jim's house.

The Sugar Creek veterinarian was at Big Jim's dad's farm that afternoon, looking after some of the animals. In fact, he was using an elastrator on the lambs' tails, which is what veterinarians do when the farmer doesn't want the tails cut off all at once. The elastrator clamps on a rubber ring very tight, which hurts the lamb a little for a few minutes and then quits hurting. About four weeks later, the tail drops off, wherever the lamb happens to be.

Circus had said he was going to have the veterinarian operate on his kitty so he would smell as fresh as a daisy instead of as fresh as a skunk.

"There are a lot of people who buy skunks for pets and pay big prices for them," Circus had told us while we were still in the middle of our excitement.

We watched until he disappeared down the lane, carrying his black and white kitty and my alarm clock.

While Poetry and I finished collecting our treasures and our thoughts, I all of a sudden heard the sound of wind in the trees. At the same time there was a roll of thunder, which meant that a Sugar Creek storm was coming up. In fact, it was almost here. The sun slid under a cloud at that very second. Then I heard another roll of thunder, which seemed closer than the other one had been.

"Wonderful!" Poetry exclaimed cheerfully. "That'll take care of your wet overalls!"

"How?" I asked, looking toward the cloudy sky.

"All you have to do is to try to get home before it rains and not quite make it. After you get yourself wet all over, your parents will blame the rain."

It was an idea, but for some reason I didn't like it.

4

There's nothing much more interesting for a boy to see than a Sugar Creek thunderstorm coming up. The sky that afternoon was wonderful to look at. Great big fierce-looking clouds, some of them almost half as big as the whole northwest part of the sky, were rolling and tumbling and tossing themselves around as if they were terribly angry. Also, savage-looking, pitchfork shaped flashes of yellow lightning were leaping from one cloud to another. Some clouds were blue-green and some were black. In the direction of our house, the sky was still clear and blue, but it wouldn't be very long.

We didn't have time to decide what we wanted to do. We had to do something quick or get wetter than two drowned rats—a large rolypoly one and a kind of skinny freckle-faced one. We were closer to Poetry's house than we were to mine, and a lot closer to their toolshed than to their house or barn.

"Come on," Poetry ordered. "We can just make it to the toolshed. Let's get these books in so they won't get wet."

A second later, carrying our stuff, we were racing ahead of the storm and through the woods toward the log cabin toolshed. When I got to the fallen log where Circus's black and white animal had been, I leaped over it and ran even faster than Poetry did, getting to the shed first and shoving the door open. That is, I started to shove the door open—and couldn't.

"It's locked," Poetry puffed behind me. "We keep it locked so people can't get in and borrow things and never bring them back."

Just then I felt a drop of rain on my one hand and about six on the other, and I knew the storm was already there. The wind in the trees was louder now, and the thunder was crashing and acting as if it really meant business. In another minute the rain would be pouring down as hard as if Sugar Creek itself was up there in the sky and someone had punched a million holes through its bed and it was leaking through every hole. And we were under it.

"Quick," Poetry puffed again. "Around on the other side there is a hole where we can crawl under. Mama Skunk and her family will be happy to have company. Come on!" He grabbed me by an arm and started to pull me along after him.

"Stop!" I thundered at the same time the sky did and jerked myself loose. If I could have seen Poetry's face, I would have known he was only fooling. A second later he shoved one of his roly-poly hands into one of his pockets, pulled out a key on a little chain, and with it unlocked the toolshed door—just in time.

The minute we were inside that dark log house, it began to rain hard and to hail. The sound was as though a hundred carpenters were up on that clapboard roof driving nails with two hundred hammers—one hammer in each hand.

I was surprised that there wasn't a bad odor inside, but there wasn't, maybe because most of the time skunks don't smell like skunks. They belong to the cat family and, like house cats and raccoons, like to keep themselves as clean as they can. In fact, they are so clean that when they get through digging up a nice fat grub— or a june bug, while it is still a grub—they stop and shake themselves to get the dirt or dust off their pretty, glossy fur before they dig again.

Well, while the rain was coming down like that and we couldn't do anything else, we looked around at Poetry's dad's farm machinery, such as an oat seeder, a drill, a cultivator, and other different things farmers use.

"Abraham Lincoln was born in a house like this," Poetry said. "Let's go up in the loft and imagine ourselves to be part of the Lincoln family."

I remembered an old joke and said, "Abe was a wonderful man; he was so wonderful he even built the house he was born in."

But Poetry didn't get the joke. He'd put down his stuff and was already on his way up a little ladder to the loft. The ladder was only a row of stout sticks driven into the wall. Pretty soon we were both up there in the half dark. There was only one window, and it wasn't very clean.

"I've been waiting for a chance to show you something. Wait until I get a light," Poetry said. With that, he shoved his hand into his pocket again and brought out the waterproof match-box he nearly always carried. He struck a match and went to a table where there was an old-fashioned kerosene lantern, which he quickly lighted. And what to my wondering eyes should appear but a nice little loft room all fixed up like a boy's den.

"Sh!" Poetry said. "This is a secret; don't tell anybody. It's just for you and me."

There was a neat little wood table and beside it a four-shelf bookcase with a lot of old books. Also there were a few pictures on the wall and two rocking chairs that he had proba-bly gotten out of the attic of his grandmother's house. On the floor was a rug that I remem-bered having seen at their house just before it got too worn for his mother to want it any-more.

Against one of the log walls was an army cot with an Indian blanket on it and a red leather cushion and a lot of other things such as an old hand-wind phonograph and a few records. On the table beside it was his green fishing tackle box, which had more lures in it than any box I ever saw.

We had to yell to each other to be heard above the rain and the hail on the roof, but be-ing in a place like that gave me a great feeling.

Poetry, being my almost best friend, made

me solemnly promise I wouldn't tell even one of the rest of the gang about it, and I promised.

"But how about Wally?" I asked. "He'll be here a whole week—he and Alexander the Copper-smith."

I don't know how long we stayed in the old house, talking and planning things to do when Wally came, while it still rained.

Before we left, Poetry got what he said was a wonderful idea. "It's the best idea I ever had in my life," he said. He wouldn't tell me what it was —just that it was an idea and I'd have to trust him.

"Remember, it's a secret," he said, "so don't tell a soul." But all he would tell me anyway was that he and Wally and I would all sleep in his tent some night, and at midnight we'd go on a little visit to the log cabin loft.

When I got home that afternoon I felt pret-ty bad that my new overalls had gotten all wet, but there wasn't a thing I could do except hope Mom or Dad or both wouldn't say very much about it.

I started to whistle as I came up to "Theodore Collins" on our mailbox and was still whistling when I got to Theodore Collins at the barn, where he had just finished milking old Brindle, our one-eared cow.

Dad was coming out the door at the time. His gray eyes under his bushy eyebrows swept over me from the top of my bare red head to the toes of my bare feet, then stopped at my wrinkled still-wet new overalls.

I was trying to act very businesslike, as if I was in a hurry to get the eggs gathered. I would have to go past him to get through the barn door. Once inside, I would climb the ladder to the haymow where old Bentcomb, my favorite hen, always laid her egg in a special nest under a log. She laid three hundred eggs last year, which is almost one a day.

But for some reason Dad's eyes were just like a pair of strong arms holding me, and I couldn't move.

I could talk, though, and did, saying, "It's Wally's fault. I did it for him."

"Your cousin Wally hasn't arrived yet. He won't be here for four weeks."

"He's here in my mind. He's been on my mind all day."

Well, Dad was sometimes a very mischievous dad, and he was always surprising me by hardly noticing something I did that was wrong, especially if he knew it was an accident. His eyes let loose of my overalls and caught me again by my own eyes, as he said with a little sarcastic mischief in his voice, "So Wally's been on your mind all day?"

"Yes," I said.

Then Dad chuckled a friendly chuckle and in a deep, friendly voice said, "Well, son, don't let him fall off. That's a pretty small place for a boy to be." Right that second his eyes stopped looking at me, and his nose started sniffing the air. "There's a skunk around here somewhere, I think. Smell it?" he asked.

I quickly turned my head in several directions, sniffing with each turn.

Then he said, "Let's be sure to close the chicken house door tonight. We can't afford to lose any of our nice laying hens."

I answered, "I smelled one of them myself about an hour ago, just before the storm. Everything smells worse when there's humidity in the air." I had heard Mom say that maybe a hundred times when the wind blew some of the barnyard odors toward our house.

"Well, you hurry up and get your eggs gathered. Mother will have supper ready pretty soon."

He started toward the house, and Mixy, who probably couldn't smell polecats as well as she could milk, followed along behind and beside and in front of him, meowing hungrily all the way.

Watching her, I thought, *Go on, little innocent cat, enjoy your happy-go-lucky life while you can. Pretty soon your fun will be over, and you'll have to watch every minute to keep from being chewed to pieces by a city dog.*

As I went into the barn and started up the ladder to the haymow, I thought I smelled a black and white kitty myself. I knew I had when, twenty minutes later, I went into the house with the eggs.

Mom, who had the kitchen full of the wonderful odor of freshly baked baking powder biscuits and raw-fried potatoes, whirled around as if a polecat had suddenly walked in. She came sniffing straight toward me. "Bill Collins!" she exclaimed. "Where have you been? You've got polecat all over you! Outside with you, young man! I don't want my house all smelled up, with your Aunt Belle coming."

"They aren't coming for four weeks yet. Four whole weeks."

"Quick! Outside! Eggs and all, until we see whether you have contaminated them too!"

And with Mom helping me by opening the door with her hands and pushing me with her voice, I started out. Then I caught one of my toes in one of my overall legs. A second later, when I came to, I was half on and half off the board walk that runs from the house to the iron pitcher pump. There were scrambled eggs all around me and on me. There were transparent whites and orange yolks and white and brown shells scattered in a mixed-up mess everywhere—on the walk, on the ground, some of them on the pump platform seven feet away. But it seemed most of them were on me—on my hands and face and all over the front of my new, wrinkled, wet overalls.

And that was how I got to take off those wet wrinkled overalls and put on a clean pair without Mom even finding out what had happened. Also, that's why, for some reason, I got to take a bath before supper, not getting to take it in the bathtub but in a washtub in our toolhouse. Dad helped me by using a special no-odor soap, which made me smell almost as bad as I did before.

5

The morning finally came when Wally and Alexander the Coppersmith arrived. I hadn't known that long-handled name was the name Wally had given to his mongrel dog until my red aunt called him that in a letter to Mom. My "red aunt" was my red-haired dad's only sister, who was also Wally's mother. We always called her my "red aunt" when we talked about her at our house. She liked that name herself, since she was a very human being, like my parents, and wasn't too dignified or stuck-up or anything.

I was standing near the walnut tree beside the mailbox when I saw their car coming down the gravel road, stirring up clouds of white dust, which the wind carried out across Dragonfly's dad's cornfield toward Bumblebee Hill. (That was Strawberry Hill's other name, and on the top of it was the old abandoned cemetery where we had so many of our gang meetings and where Old Man Paddler's wife and his boys were buried.)

It was almost noon, and Mom had lunch ready, and I was as hungry as a bear. That means I was as hungry as a boy who is in good health and has had an early breakfast and nothing to eat since—except for maybe a few strawberries he has found on Strawberry Hill, a few wild raspberries from a row of bushes along the border of Dragonfly's cornfield, and maybe a slice of bread and butter and grape jam that he has talked his mother into letting him have.

I was feeling pretty sad, as well as hungry, still thinking about my week of torture that was just ahead and still remembering the last time my dad and I had talked it over, which was that very morning. We had been out by the grape arbor at the time, where we had stretched a little canvas for Alexander the Coppersmith to sleep under at night.

"After all, William," Dad began, calling me by my hated name, "Wally's parents are entitled to a little vacation. Every husband and his wife ought to have at least a week each year somewhere away from their children, if they want it, just to give themselves a little variety in life and a little rest. Your Aunt Belle has never seen the Black Hills nor the Rockies, and so, since your Uncle Amos has his vacation at this time, we are cooperating with them and taking Wally off their hands."

"And putting him on my hands," I said.

"You forget," Dad explained, and again he was using friendly sarcasm, "your mother and I have on our hands a red-haired freckle-faced boy of our own all year, so we can sympathize with Wally's parents."

I knew he was only joking, but not being in the mood for a joke when I was in the middle of it, I didn't laugh.

As I told you, we were standing beside the grape arbor at the time. I looked away and up and, seeing the two-by-four crossbeam just above my head, jumped up, caught it in both hands, swung myself into a skin-the-cat movement, and in a jiffy was sitting on top, feeling a little better because I had used my muscles to let off a little red-haired steam.

"You may discover that Wally is a pretty good boy after all," he said. "You have to get acquainted with people to understand them. You have to get into their minds to do that."

Well, when the Sensenbrenners' car came swinging in through the gate I had opened for them, stopped beside the plum tree, and Wally and his dog came tumbling out, I knew that my time of reckoning had come. He and Alexander the Coppersmith had been riding in the backseat. The very second the car stopped, the back door was thrust open, and both he and his mongrel dog came tumbling out at the same time. They got tangled up with each other as they came, and Wally stumbled and fell and rolled out onto the lawn.

One reason he had a hard time getting out was that he was trying to bring out with him a twenty-four- by thirty-six-inch mattress, which accidentally fell under him. That was the reason he didn't get hurt the very first minute he was on our farm.

"What on earth?" I exclaimed.

My red aunt, hearing me, said, "My son and your cousin are on the earth," and she laughed a musical laugh. In spite of her being a woman, her laugh reminded me of Dad's, and I could tell they were brother and sister.

Just that minute, from the direction of the house I heard Mom's voice calling a cheerful welcome. A second after that, the side door slammed as loud as I sometimes let it slam myself when I go out in a hurry on my way to somewhere or other. Then I heard Mom say what she nearly always says when we have company she likes and hasn't seen for a while: "Well, well, my, my, and for land's sakes! Come on in!"

I couldn't resist saying mischievously to Mom, "You can go back and shut that door like a gentleman," quoting what I had heard Dad say quite a few hundred times in my life. But Mom was too pleased to see Uncle Amos and Aunt Belle to care what I said.

The first thing I noticed about my Uncle Amos as soon as he slid out from under the cream-colored steering wheel and came around to let Mom hug him the way she does all our relatives when they come, was that he had three eyebrows—one above each of his two brown eyes and the other on his upper lip just below his long nose. He had a deep businesslike voice.

And as Dad and Mom and my red aunt and her three-eyebrowed husband told each other how glad they were to see each other, hardly noticing me at all, Wally and especially Alexander the Coppersmith started taking over the place.

In a second, the dog was running all over

the yard, smelling everything and acting as if he had the heebie-jeebies. And then, as quick as a flash, I heard the rush of flying feet, which sounded like an excited wind with a bad cold. I looked around just in time to see a streak of black and white flashing from our side porch toward the grape arbor and a faster flash of copper streaking after it.

Boy oh boy, did Mixy ever run! She went up the round grape-arbor post like a streak of greased lightning. A second later, she was on the two-by-four crossbeam, and Wally's mongrel was below with his tongue hanging out and panting and barking and jumping up and scratching at the corner post and acting as if there was any one thing he couldn't stand in his dog world more than anything else, it was a black and white cat.

Anyway, that was the first two and one-half minutes of Wally's visit, and there was a whole week ahead, with sixty minutes in each hour and twenty-four hours in a day and seven whole days before the week would finally be over. That would be ten thousand and eighty whole minutes—and each minute would have sixty seconds in it!

Thinking of that reminded me of my alarm clock and of another black and white kitty. Circus had saved the clock for me, and, after a few days of airing and oiling, it smelled like an alarm clock again. Right that second it was in my room upstairs, ticking off the minutes for me as fast as it could count.

Oh, well, I thought, *the week is started anyway, and seven days from now it will all be over.* Only there would be seven nights too, with a dog barking all night and a boy snoring and—but remembering Poetry's and my plans to take Wally some night to our den in the loft of the toolshed, which had a family of skunks living under it, I sighed a sigh of worried relief.

At least Wally wasn't in favor of what Alexander was doing. He untangled himself from himself and yelled across the yard, saying, "Alexander, stop that!" And picking up the mattress, he started on a good fast run toward the grape arbor. On the way he had to pass the board walk, which was slightly elevated. Looking over the top of his mattress at Alexander, he didn't see the walk, and the next thing I heard was a tangled-up scramble of feet, and Wally went down *ker-floppety-fluff-fluff* on top of his mattress again.

"That boy!" My red aunt sighed anxiously. "I hope you folks live through the week. I hope *he* lives through it."

And Uncle Amos said from under his third eyebrow, "It's a good thing he brought his dog mattress along to fall down on, so he won't break his neck."

By the time Wally had gotten up again, Mixy had decided the grape arbor wasn't a safe place. She streaked across the barnyard, followed by a barking copper-colored dog, scattering chickens in every direction as she hurried to the hole under the barn where she knew she would be safe.

And that was the first three and one-half minutes of Wally the Whirlwind's visit. There were only ten thousand seventy-six and one-half more minutes, and the week would be history.

"What's the mattress for?" I asked Wally.

He answered, "For Alexander to sleep on. It's chemically treated to keep off fleas and ticks and nits and keep him off the ground when he sleeps. He gets nervous if he is bothered by fleas, and it's not good for a dog to be nervous. It also helps to keep him from smelling like a dog. I brought his no-odor dog biscuits too, which we feed him every day. So don't you dare give him anything else to eat while he is here. They've got chlorophyll in them."

"What's that?" I asked.

"Don't you know? Didn't you ever hear of chlorophyll? But of course, you probably wouldn't —you live out in the sticks. I mean, you live in the country, and you wouldn't know about such things. It is a new scientific discovery which is put in dog food, and it deodorizes a dog so he won't smell like a dog."

So, I thought and felt my temper rising. *I live out in the sticks, do I? And I wouldn't know, would I?* I decided to act as ignorant as I knew he thought I was and as I knew he was. So I asked, "So he won't smell like a dog—or he won't smell like a dog smells?"

Well, it was time for lunch for sure, because

Wally's parents were in a hurry to get started to the Black Hills, hoping to get a few hundred miles farther before night.

Wally screamed for Alexander the Coppersmith to come back and leave Mixy alone, calling and scolding in a tone of voice that, if I had been a dog, I would have resented. It would have made me not want to come.

But—would you believe it?—that dog actually obeyed him. He came trotting toward the iron pitcher pump where we were, wagging his tail happily as though he was proud of himself for having chased a big, fierce, wild black and white cat, having saved all our lives by doing it.

Wally quick pulled a leather leash out of his hip pocket, snapped one end to Alexander's collar, which had on its nameplate "Alexander the Coppersmith, Property of Walford Sensenbrenner, 222 Sunset Boulevard, Memory City, Indiana," and tied the other end to the grape arbor post.

Then all of us went in to eat. Wally and I had to be reminded to wash our hands first, "To get the dog smell off," Mom said cheerfully.

I said to her from the bathroom door, "We don't have any on our hands. Alexander isn't that kind of a dog."

"Wash your hands," Mom repeated, half singing the command so it wouldn't sound like she probably felt.

As soon as our clean hands were washed, we all gathered around the table—Mom and

Dad and Uncle Amos and Aunt Belle and Charlotte Ann, my baby sister, and Wally and me. Charlotte Ann was sitting in her high chair between our parents, and Wally and I were on a bench on one side of the table along the south wall of the room.

Pretty soon, when it was as quiet as it could get with the teakettle singing on the stove, a lot of happy old hens singing just outside the door, Alexander the Coppersmith already barking at something, and different farm noises coming in from the barn, Dad said, "The Collins family will ask the blessing together," which is what he always says when he wants us to sing the blessing.

Right away he started off with the melody of a little chorus that had the tune of one of our church songs. As soon as I found the pitch, Mom joined with an alto, he switched to the tenor, and, if I do say so, the harmony sounded as pretty as anything. The words were:

We thank Thee, Lord, for this our food,
For life and health and every good;
These mercies bless, and grant that we
May feast in Paradise with Thee. Amen.

After we sang, "Amen," my dad said an especially good prayer, asking the Lord to bless us all and especially Uncle Amos and Aunt Belle on their trip to the West. Part of his prayer was, "We thank Thee for the beautiful world Thou hast given us. Let this time of vacation be one of refreshment for their hearts and minds as well as for their bodies. And may they see in the hills and mountains and the other wonderful things of nature the hand of God, who loves us all, who gave His Son to die for our sins."

He also prayed that Wally's vacation would be a happy one "in the fresh country air and because of the outdoor exercise which is so good for a growing boy."

My mind had a hard time staying with the prayer because "fresh country air" reminded me of Poetry's toolshed, and "exercise" reminded me of potato hoeing and chores of a thousand kinds to do. I couldn't imagine Wally's being interested in that kind of exercise.

When the prayer was finished, I opened my eyes and took a quick look at the fried chicken and the other food that I had been smelling for what seemed a long time. I also looked at my red aunt and noticed she had tears in her blue-green eyes and a very reverent expression on her face.

"Thank you, Theo," she said. "That's like it used to be in the old home—" She stopped and swallowed something in her throat, which she hadn't eaten, and started again. "You three sing together nicely. Where did you get your voice, Bill—from your mother or your father?"

Wally answered, trying to be funny and not being, "From one of the crows out in the woods."

If my friend Poetry or another of the gang had said that, I'd have thought it was cute. But when Wally's mind thought of it and his sarcastic voice said it, I didn't think it was humorous.

Uncle Amos didn't think so either, because I saw his two upper eyebrows drop and heard a sharp voice from under his other eyebrow say, "That's enough!" And the tone of voice reminded me of Wally himself yelling out across the barnyard at Alexander the Coppersmith to stop barking at Mixy.

As soon as the meal was over, everybody went out to the car, and Uncle Amos and my red aunt got in to drive away. Wally took his suitcase out of the car's trunk and a large carton of no-odor dog biscuits and a baseball, a bat and glove, a fishing rod and reel, and a tackle box.

Uncle Amos drove past the plum tree and out into the barnyard, scaring our chickens and scattering them. Then he turned around and came back, stopping once more where he had been, and said through the open window, "We'll drop you postcards along the way."

My red aunt said to Wally, "Be a good boy, Wally, and have a nice vacation."

Uncle Amos added one more command to Wally: "And leave some of the farm and neighborhood for others to enjoy after you are through with them."

Well, that was the first sixty minutes of Wally's week. There were more than ten thousand more worried minutes to suffer through.

The very second the car started to pull out of the drive, there was a noise as if the world was about to come to an end up near the grape arbor. I looked and saw a copper-colored dog running wild in six or seven directions and straining at his leash. The whole grape arbor was shaking as though there was an earthquake.

In the middle of the excitement I also saw the collar slide over and off the dog's head. Then, faster than greased lightning, a blurred streak of copper shot over the board walk and out across the yard to the gate, past "Theodore Collins" on the mailbox, and down the road after Uncle Amos's cream-and-green car, getting to the left front wheel before the car could pick up speed.

There was a wild and excited barking and also Uncle Amos's voice barking out of his open window, "Alexander! Stop it!" And from beside or behind me or from somewhere, Wally's voice started yelling, using the same words his father used, calling Alexander to stop and to come back.

Then the car sped up as though it was in a race and shot down that road at sixty miles an hour, leaving Alexander far behind.

In only about a minute, the dog got discouraged. Anyway, with Wally calling him, he started back, stopping every now and then to smell different things along the roadside. But when I saw his smiling dog face and his hanging-out tongue, I decided he wasn't discouraged at all. He seemed very happy. It was just as if he was saying, "There, see what I did! I not only scared the daylights out of a wild, dangerous black and white cat, but I chased a great big four-wheeled car clear out of the neighborhood. They're all scared of me!"

"Come on, Wally," I said. "Let's get started on the next ten thousand minutes."

"Get started on the next ten thousand what?" Dad asked.

I answered, "Maybe we ought to get the dishes washed, just in case some of the gang come over and want to help hoe potatoes or something."

I let my eyes meet my dad's for a moment, and he winked at me with his left one. "That's an idea," he said. "You boys help Mother with the dishes, and then, if the gang comes, you'll be all set to go swimming. We won't do too much work on Wally's first day here."

I looked doubtfully at him, just as Wally said, "I'll get my swimsuit out of the suitcase." He started to open it right there in the front yard.

Mom stopped him by saying, "Wait. Bill, you help carry things up to his room. The two top drawers in the bureau are empty for his shirts and things."

We stopped at the grape arbor on the way while Wally put Alexander's collar back on. Wally tightened it one more notch and checked the other end to be sure it was tied tight to the grape arbor post, because you could never tell when Mixy might decide to come innocently past on her way to somewhere or other.

Right that second, I heard a noise out by the walnut tree, and, looking back, I saw a barrel-shaped boy just opening the mailbox. It was good old Poetry himself, wearing a red shirt. I had just told Poetry on the phone that very day that he needn't stop for me because I probably couldn't go swimming with the gang, anyway.

"Hi, Poetry!" I yelled to him as he came waddling across the yard toward where all our excitement was. He was welcomed by Mom, who acted happy to see him. Alexander the Coppersmith also welcomed him by acting as if he had never seen anyone like him before and said so with a growl in his throat.

Wally had only half liked Poetry the last time he'd been here. When he saw who it was, he said the same thing he had said the other time, "Well, well, well, if it isn't Little Red Riding Hood."

Poetry, who was the best make-believe player of our whole gang, answered by saying the same thing *he* had said the last time, "And what big teeth you have, Grandma."

Wally's big front teeth *were* too large for his small red head, as lots of boys' teeth are until they get older and their heads grow a little more.

Alexander the Coppersmith kept on growling and eyeing Poetry suspiciously.

"I brought my wolf along this time," Wally said. "Want to come and pet him?"

Poetry walked toward Alexander and stopped about five feet from the end of his leash.

"It's a dog," I said.

"Is that so?" Poetry said. "I couldn't tell for sure."

Mom, who by that time was out by the plum tree talking with Dad, called, "Better get Wally's luggage upstairs right away."

Poetry and Wally followed me inside. Wally came last, letting the screen door slam hard after him. They followed me across the worn kitchen linoleum to the dining room and upstairs.

Poetry had been there hundreds of times, but Wally had been there only once, so he looked around as if he had never seen anything like it. First, he looked up at the ceiling of the biggest and longest room, where my dad had stretched about fifteen feet of chicken yard wire and put on it several layers of his finest seed corn. He always kept his fanciest seed corn there in the winter and sometimes some of it in the summer. Sometimes Dad gets blue ribbons at the fairs and horse shows that we have around the country.

We got Wally's stuff unpacked in the smaller room at the other end of the hall from mine. My room was the longest one on the south side and had an ivy vine covering almost half of the window. On a moonlit night, I always liked to look under that ivy out at the barn and the garden and across the fields to the houses of the different members of the gang. I also liked to listen to the friendly rustling of the big glossy leaves that grew in stems of five all over it and covered almost half of the whole south side of the house.

That's one of the finest sounds a boy ever hears—ivy leaves whispering in the moonlight. In the summer I nearly always went to sleep at night listening to them.

"What's the corn up there for?" Wally asked.

I explained. "That's my dad's fancy seed corn. The rats and mice can't get at it up there. It's worth hundreds of dollars, and he can't run the risk of letting some mouse or rat start gnawing on it, so he keeps it up there. Rats and mice can't climb bare walls."

Wally looked around at the unpapered, white plastered walls and asked, astonished, "You mean there are rats and mice up here?"

"Could be. Want to hear one?" I walked over to the attic door and swung it open. "Come here and just listen a minute. Hear that?" I winked at Poetry, and he started scratching with his fingernail on the wall beside the attic door.

But Wally caught on right away. "Such big rats!" he said. Then he looked into the attic, where there were a hundred different things that weren't any good but which Mom didn't like to throw away, such as the old-fashioned red cradle she had been rocked in when she was a baby and a twelve-barreled candle mold, which her great-great-grandparents had used to make candles when they were alive on this earth.

"What's *that*?" Wally asked when I picked up the candle mold and turned it over in my hands.

"My great-great-great-grandparents used it to make candles when this part of America was just being born."

"Humph," he said. "Country people certainly didn't have much that was modern."

That kind of fired me up, so I said, "They certainly didn't, but they were pretty nice people. Some of their city descendants aren't always as nice." Then I shut the attic door and said to Poetry, "I thought I told you on the phone not to bother—"

"Your father called back right after we finished talking and told me to come. He said to come over and help you."

"Help me do what?"

"He didn't say—just come and help you."

"Can't we go swimming first?" Wally asked, probably figuring there was some work that would have to be done.

Just then I heard a strange noise outside, which I knew wasn't coming from the barn. Looking out, I saw Alexander the Coppersmith making a lot of excited noise in the direction of the walnut tree.

Then I saw five boys coming across the lot. The tall brown-haired boy with an almost mustache on his upper lip was Big Jim, our leader. Another almost as tall boy, who right that second was turning a handspring, was Circus, our acrobat. A short, spindle-legged little guy, who right that second was looking up toward the sky to get sunlight in his eyes to help him finish a sneeze he was having trouble finishing, was

Dragonfly, the pop-eyed member, who is allergic to practically everything. Beside Big Jim was a cute, curly headed guy, the smallest and youngest and best member, Little Jim himself. I watched him walk straight toward the iron pitcher pump, where he started to pump some water. He probably was thirsty.

A great big glad feeling started racing all through me and up and down my spine. If Dad had called Poetry to come, he had also probably asked all the members of the gang to come. And even with Wally there, it was going to be a lot of fun to be with the gang. I felt so good I could have chased a wildcat across our barnyard myself.

"Come on," I said to Wally and Poetry. "Let's get down and get going. It won't be so bad after all, maybe. There are only about nine thousand nine hundred and fifty left."

"Nine thousand nine hundred and fifty *what?*" Wally asked.

I answered, "Nothing," and swished toward the banister and went downstairs two steps at a time.

6

We had a grand time swimming that afternoon, although for some reason I didn't feel as happy as usual. I kept worrying all the time because of Wally and Alexander the Coppersmith's not having very good country manners and wondering what the gang would think of me for having such strange relatives.

I discovered, though, that the dog had already been trained to retrieve a stick Wally would throw. He would race madly after it, catch it up in his mouth, and come galloping proudly back with it, acting as pleased as a boy carrying home a good report card to his parents, who probably didn't expect him to have even one good grade because of his not being as smart as they remembered they were when they were his age.

Anyway, it was as easy as pie to teach Alexander to dash wildly out into Sugar Creek after a stick we'd throw in. He acted as if he didn't even know water was water or that he was getting himself all wet. Of course, he didn't have to worry about what his mother would think when he got home. But the very second he reached shore, he would shake himself to get the water out of his ears and off him. Anybody and everybody who was near him would get a free shower.

Once, after Alexander had come splashing back with a stick, he stopped right beside Circus and showered water all over him. That made Circus exclaim, "Hey, you dumb dog, these are my brand-new overalls! Don't you know anything?"

I looked at Circus, and he did have on a brand-new pair of blue bib overalls. In fact, I had noticed them when I'd first seen Circus doing handsprings across our yard. I hadn't said anything and had pretended not to notice, because it might have been embarrassing for him.

Circus's parents had so many children, especially girls, to buy clothes for. How they managed to scrape together enough money to get clothes for them all, I don't know. Anyway, sometimes Circus had patches in a half-dozen places on his clothes, and sometimes there were even patches on the patches themselves. That goes to show that somebody in his family knew how to sew.

But Dragonfly didn't always think before he spoke. "Where'd you get the money to pay for them?" he asked.

If I had known he was going to say that, I'd have clapped my hand over his mouth. Circus was another one of my almost best friends, and I didn't want him to be embarrassed because his folks were poor.

But Circus, instead of acting hurt in his heart, just grinned and answered, "Oh, that was easy—I sold my black and white kitty. I got enough to buy a pair of shoes and a Sunday shirt and had enough left to put ten dollars in the bank—all for one black and white woods cat!"

We had finished swimming and were getting ready to go back through the tall weeds to the little brown footpath that winds along the creek from the swimming hole to the spring. From the spring we were going to the old sycamore tree and on up to Old Man Paddler's cabin in the hills.

Wally's curiosity was so aroused about the black and white kitty that he kept asking questions as we walked along. So Circus told him the whole story about catching the little skunk by the tail, plopping him into a milk can, and taking him to the veterinarian for an operation. He wound up by saying, "A rich lady in the city wanted him for a house pet, so I sold him to her for twenty-five dollars."

We'd reached the spring and were lying down resting in the warm sunshine by the old black widow stump before Circus—with Poetry and me helping him—finally finished his kitty story.

"Want to hear a poem about a polecat?" Poetry asked and was halfway through before Dragonfly, who didn't like Poetry's poetry, stopped him.

But Wally's curiosity was really aroused. "You mean, all you have to do to catch a skunk is to sneak up on it and pick it up by the tail, and you can sell it for twenty-five dollars?"

"Bill and Poetry saw me do it—didn't you?"

"Sure," Poetry said and winked across the top of a bell-shaped purplish flower that was growing between our faces—a bluebell, I think it was.

I caught the meaning of his wink and the mischievous look on his face, and I said to Wally, "Sure."

"But didn't he smell after you caught him?"

"Oh, maybe a little," Circus said.

Well, putting that idea in Wally's mind was just like planting an onion seed in our garden.

"I've got a whole hundred dollars in the bank at home. I save every cent I can," he said.

And I could see that he had his mind made up to make twenty-five dollars himself before his week was up and my Uncle Amos and my red aunt came back from their happy vacation, which would be the end of their carefree life.

It felt good to lie there in the tall bluegrass in that warm sunshine after staying in the water almost too long and getting cold. Little Jim was getting blue lips and shivering before we'd all decided we had been in long enough.

So, as we always like to do, we lay there sprawled in a half-dozen different directions, feeling happy.

While I was stretched out on my back, I sort of let my mind drift away like the big white cumulus cloud that was hanging up there in the blue Sugar Creek sky, just over the top of the leaning linden tree above the spring. *It would be nice to have five hundred dollars in the bank,* I thought. I already had one hundred dollars but didn't say so because that was perhaps the first ten dollars Circus had ever saved. It must have seemed pretty wonderful to him.

I couldn't help but remember that this was the place where Circus's dad—when he was still an alcoholic—had gotten bit by a black widow spider, which is how the stump got its name. He had to go to the hospital and almost died. But while he was there he began to think about the kind of life he had been living, and after that he became a Christian. Ever since, he had been a different person, and he and Circus's mother and all the rest of the family went to church every Sunday.

As I kept on looking up toward the sky, I thought for a minute that it was the Lord Himself who had made the sky and the white clouds and the shining green leaves on the trees and such things as bluebells and dogtooth violets. I thought that He must like beautiful things and pretty sounds such as the chattering water in Sugar Creek and the singing birds—and that every so often He gives His world a good washing in rainwater.

I was also thinking—between the noise of Alexander the Coppersmith trotting around in the leaves all about us and the gang's chattering—that only a few years ago, if Circus had made twenty-five dollars, most of it would have been put in the bank by the tavern keeper of Sugar Creek.

Just thinking that made me mad inside. I

wished I could make everybody in the world see how silly it was to trade good money for a lot of smelly stuff to pour down one's throat.

Well, that was one of the interesting things I did around Sugar Creek—just let my mind drift like a cloud in the sky while my body was lying in the warm sunshine somewhere.

But a boy's mind doesn't get to drift very long when the rest of the gang is around. Just that second, I felt something tickling my nose as if an ant was trying to crawl into one of my nostrils. I brushed at it with my hand, shut my mind's eye, and opened both my others just in time to see Poetry tickling me with the greenish blue head of a bluegrass stalk.

That was just like sticking a pin into a balloon and letting all the air out of it. I came down out of my sky to the earth, and there I was, beside the black widow stump.

Before long, all seven of us were playing leapfrog and laughing and telling stories and having fun on our way to the sycamore tree and the mouth of the cave.

Everything went smoothly until we got to the little flower-bordered lane where Circus and Poetry and I had had our interesting experience with the twenty-five dollar black and white kitty. We had to go past the toolshed on the way to the sycamore tree, and I was already beginning to smell the mother skunk and her family of six kittens who had their summer home under the shed.

I hoped we could get past without Wally

getting any ideas, but we didn't. The second we
got anywhere near the place, he stopped stock-
still and sniffed. All of a sudden, Alexander the
Coppersmith did the same thing. Then he
started acting excited, as though he could
hardly stand the strange smell that was coming
into the two nostrils of his cold black nose. (All
dogs have cold noses when they are in good
health and hot ones when they are sick.)

I don't know what a skunk smells like to a
dog that has never smelled one before—
whether it is like perfume is to a lady and he
can't stand *not* to smell more of it or what. But
that dog started acting like a dog that had gone
crazy. He had his cold nose to the ground over
by the fallen stump and was sniffing all around
it and on top of it and was acting wild.

Then, like a copper flash, he was off on a
zigzagging trail in the direction of the toolshed. He got there in only a few seconds. Then
he let loose with his insane voice, which sounded like half an excited bark, about one-third a
worried whine, and the rest of it an invitation
to whatever he was barking at to just show up
once and it would be the last of him forever.

From behind me, Wally cried, "It's a skunk!
Let's go see him!" He started on the run toward the toolshed.

It wasn't easy to stop what was about to happen. I knew that any minute Alexander would
dive under that toolshed and come out with
one of the black and white kitties—or else
come out the way I had seen Circus's dad's

hounds do when they accidentally or on purpose got into a scrap with one. They would come out rolling and twisting and turning somersaults in the grass.

It was Circus who stopped Wally by saying, "We don't even dare try to catch one of them without putting it in something. They are pretty savage if they get mad at you. You *have* to have something to put them in."

So Wally quickly grabbed Alexander by the collar. With Poetry and me also holding onto his collar, we stopped him from going under the toolshed. But I knew that if the mother skunk happened to be outside and came back and found us there, we might find ourselves in a fight with the whole family!

Wally wasn't satisfied, though, and neither was Alexander the Coppersmith. Wally left the toolshed with a stubborn look on his face. He had been stopped from doing something he wanted to do, and I could see he wasn't used to that.

"I am going to get me a pet skunk before I leave," he said. "I want him all nice and tame by the time my folks get back, so they'll let me take him home."

Alexander the Coppersmith's face was just as stubborn, and I had a feeling that, the very first time he got a chance, he would show everybody he wasn't afraid of anybody's black and white kitty out in the woods.

On we finally went. Nothing exciting happened until after we had had our visit with Old

Man Paddler in his Abraham Lincoln style cabin. Something he told us just before we left introduced us to a brand-new danger—one we hadn't had in the Sugar Creek territory, and it scared me half to smithereens. And if Alexander the Coppersmith hadn't been along when the new danger happened, if he hadn't been such a dumb dog and not scared of anything, including fierce four-footed animals, somebody would have been killed for sure. Boy oh boy, talk about hair-raising adventures! I had a little more respect for Alexander the Coppersmith after that experience.

7

Old Man Paddler must have been expecting us. He had his little two-burner folding camp stove already going, and steam was pouring from the teakettle. He used a little gasoline stove in the summertime instead of heating up his big, old-fashioned, wood-and-coal-burning range.

In only a minute or two, we would all be drinking sassafras tea, which is what the kind old man always made for us when we came to see him. Little Jim liked it better than any other drink. "It's just like melted lollipops," he always said.

While we were waiting for the little red chips of sassafras roots to boil a while longer in a white enamel stewpan, Wally kept looking all around the room, letting his eyes stop for a second or two on the different things that a city boy hardly ever gets to see.

Without looking myself, I knew just what he was seeing, because I had been in the old man's house so many times. He was seeing the old-fashioned stairs leading up to the loft, the big embossed motto on the wall above the fireplace with the Bible verse on it that said, "For by grace you have been saved through faith; and that not of yourselves, it is the gift of God."

Also he was probably seeing the little hospital-type bed against the wall and the old-fashioned kerosene lamp and the new gas lamp on the shelf above the fireplace. On another wall was a muzzle-loading gun, which the old man had probably used when he was a boy or a young man, and just below it was a beautiful walnut-stocked bolt-action Winchester .22 rifle with a checkered butt plate.

I looked at Wally's face just about the time his eyes hit that rifle, and I saw them light up. I guessed that he was wishing he had one like that himself, which is what nearly every boy in the world wishes he could have.

Pretty soon the tea and cookies were ready. The cookies were the ones Mom had me take to Old Man Paddler a few days ago, and the cooky jar was one the gang had given him on his birthday. I will never forget how pleased he was when he unwrapped that cooky jar. His gray eyes had twinkled as he said, "If your mothers will keep it filled, it will always have cookies in it when you come to see me." And, for some reason, nearly every week some of our mothers baked a batch of cookies for him, which we took up to his cabin. Imagine that! Having to walk all the way up into the hills just to take a batch of cookies to an old man who probably didn't eat even half of them himself!

Knowing that he always asked the blessing before he ate anything, even if it was only an afternoon snack, all the gang quieted down from what we were saying and doing and were as still as six mice. Wally, not expecting anything like that and noticing how quiet we were, looked around at our half-sober faces with his puzzled one and said, "What's the matter?"

The old man must have been expecting such a question. Anyway, he said, "I suppose God knows we are thankful for what He has done for us, but I expect to go up to see Him before long, and there's something special I want to mention to Him right away." Then he bowed his grizzled head, and Wally got a little more education that didn't hurt him any.

Just a second before I shut my eyes, I took a look at the white-whiskered old head and thought what a nice man he was.

Right away his trembling voice started praying a quiet prayer. He thanked the Lord for the Sugar Creek Gang and the food and for everything in the out-of-doors such as the birds and trees and flowers and the creek itself. As he always did, he mentioned the gang by our nicknames—Big Jim, Little Jim, Circus, Dragonfly, Poetry, and me, Bill Collins—figuring probably the Lord knew us by those names as well as the ones our parents had given us. And not knowing Wally's real name, he just called him Wally.

For a few seconds then, it seemed Old Man Paddler forgot we were there. He began to talk to the Lord about a book he was writing, which he was trying to get finished that summer, and which I knew he had already named *The Christian After Death*. Part of his prayer about the book was "Help me to leave behind something that will point a lot of other people to the Savior."

Then he did forget we were there and said, "If You happen to see my wife, Sarah, or either one of my boys who are up there somewhere, just tell them that I am all right and feeling fine and will be up as soon as You are through with me down here."

I thought I heard Wally gasp when the old man's quiet voice said that. I felt very sad for a minute myself, for if there was anything I hated to even think about, it was that the time should ever have to come when Seneth Paddler would move away from Sugar Creek. I mean when his soul would go to heaven and they would bury his body in the cemetery at the top of Bumblebee Hill.

As much as I knew he would enjoy heaven, we would miss him down here terribly. Imagine the gang's going up to his cabin on a summer day and finding the door locked and nobody home and weeds growing all around the path from the house to the spring where he got his drinking water. Or imagine going up on a winter day, and seeing no blue wood smoke coming out of the chimney and no Moseslike old man standing in the open door calling us to come on in and get warm. And nobody to make sassafras tea for us or to tell us stories about the Sugar Creek of long ago.

It certainly wouldn't seem right on Sunday morning to look across the church from where I always sat with my parents and not see his fine old head as he sat down near the front, just three rows behind the piano, which Little Jim's mom played. And Sylvia's dad couldn't call on him to pray or anything. Maybe a lot of people in the world wouldn't be as good as they were if he weren't here to pray for them.

My mind started to drift again like a cloud in a sad Sugar Creek sky, but almost right away it came back to earth because something in Old Man Paddler's prayer woke me up. It was "Don't let any serious accidents happen to the boys. Protect them all while they play and work together and while they grow toward manhood."

It was a pretty wonderful prayer, and I made up my mind that someday I would learn to pray just as good a one myself, if I could.

As hungry as I was for the cookies and as thirsty as I was for a cup of melted lollipops, I could have listened to Old Man Paddler pray a little longer without getting tired. Also, for some reason, I was thinking of my cousin Wally and was glad he was hearing what Old Man Paddler was saying. It seemed the Lord was another Person right in the room with us; we just couldn't see Him. I knew He liked all the boys and girls in the world and wanted them to enjoy all the wonderful things in nature that He had made just for them. Something the old man said in his prayer must have reminded him of something else, because a little later, while we were having our tea and cookies, he excused himself, stood up, and went over to a corner of the room. There he lifted a white cloth from a basketful of apples, saying, "You boys help yourselves to these before you go."

I had seen apples exactly like them in one of his orchards about a quarter of a mile from his cabin, where we had helped ourselves any time we wanted to—he having given us permission.

Well, when the old man said for us to help ourselves to the apples in the basket, Dragonfly spoke up and said, "We can get all we want on our way home."

"That's what I mean," Old Man Paddler answered. "I think maybe you boys won't want to climb over into the orchard today. It's not safe."

What could he mean? I wondered.

Then he told us. Just yesterday he had rented one of his pastures to a cattleman named Harm Groenwald, who had moved into the Sugar Creek neighborhood. The pasture was right next to that apple orchard. There was a big red bull running with Mr. Groenwald's other cattle, the old man said, and that very morning while he was in his orchard getting apples, the bull had spotted him. Seeing the old man and being mad about something anyway, as bulls quite often are, he had let loose a mad bellow and started crashing down the gate.

"I'm too old to hurry very fast," Old Man Paddler said. "I don't do so well since I fell down the cellar stairs. So I almost didn't make it. I did get to the other side of the orchard and over the wire fence just in time, though. If it hadn't been for the Lord helping me, I wouldn't be here this afternoon."

When he said that, it was easier to understand why he had prayed the way he had—about his going up to heaven to see his wife and boys and about us being protected from danger.

"Until we get a new bullproof gate, we'll all have to stay out of the orchard," he cautioned us. Then his old eyes spotted Poetry's red shirt. "Your shirt wouldn't help his temper any, either," he said. "A bull always sees red when he sees red."

Also he looked at Wally's and my red hair. "And there are two other reasons why you should stay on this side of the fence."

First Big Jim and then all of us thanked the old man for warning us. We knew enough about farm life to know how dangerous bulls are when they really are dangerous.

But Wally's city experience had been a lot different from ours. The very first thing he said after we left the cabin was "I want to see the bull. I never saw an honest to goodness bad-tempered one in my life."

8

Honestly, I never saw a boy and his dog get into more interesting and exciting situations and into more trouble they had to have help to get out of!

On the way to the orchard, Wally let Alexander run free, and did that mongrel enjoy his liberty! He made life miserable for every rabbit and squirrel and chipmunk he saw, making a fierce fast dash after them the minute he spied them. Once a covey of quail exploded into the air in front of his curious nose, and, as quail do, they fanned up and out in every direction. Poor Alexander was dumbfounded. He couldn't decide which direction to run. He made an excited leap into the air. Before he came down, he had turned a complete circle.

I was remembering how smart quail were. When a family of them was on the ground, they arranged themselves in a little cluster with their tails together and their heads pointing outward like the spokes of a wheel. Then when any danger came along, they could burst into the air, and their wings wouldn't get in each other's way. They'd each start off in a different direction, which would make it safer for them in case anybody shot at them.

But nothing seemed to bother Alexander

the Coppersmith very long. He was just as happy that he had chased nine or ten quail out of his sight as if they had been that many wild animals. The proud expression on his face never left for more than a few seconds at a time. When he did stop running for some reason and walk ahead of us or beside Wally for even a few seconds, he would lift his sharp-toenailed feet as proudly as if he were a fancy show horse at a county fair.

Well, pretty soon we came to the edge of the pasture Old Man Paddler had rented to Mr. Groenwald. I noticed that the cattle were up at the other end, standing in the shade of some trees near the orchard, probably in the shade of the very apple tree that had on it the apples I liked best. Also I remembered that the gate leading into the orchard was there. At that distance, my eyes couldn't separate the bull from the rest of the cattle, but I supposed he was there with them, anyway.

In the same pasture not far from where we were, there was a flock of maybe sixty sheep, quite a few of which were cute little woolly lambs. Some of them had tails and some of them not. While I was wondering if Mr. Groenwald had used an elastrator on his lambs, as most of the Sugar Creek farmers had done that year, Alexander came galloping back from having chased a rabbit out of his sight. Then he spied the flock of sheep.

One lamb was closer to the fence than the rest, and Alexander ran excitedly up and down the fence till he found an opening big enough for a dog to get through. Then away he went, head and nose and teeth first, toward that lamb, which, looking up from nibbling grass and seeing and hearing and maybe smelling Alexander coming, started to run like Little Bo Peep's sheep, carrying its tail behind it.

The lamb was bleating as it ran, and I realized it was a one-sided race in which the lamb was sure to lose.

Suddenly a covey of seven boys' voices exploded into the air and shot like bullets in the direction of that dog, each of us saying the same thing in different words: "Stop, you dumb dog!" "Stop, you crazy, nonsensical mongrel!" "Stop! Don't you know anything?" "Leave that lamb alone!"

And all the time Wally was yelling, "Alexander, stop! Alexander the Coppersmith, come back here!"

But that uncontrollable dog was like a boy in a footrace with a crowd of people yelling and rooting for him to run faster. He *didn't* stop.

I was both mad and scared. I could imagine that insane dog's sharp teeth tearing the lamb's shoulder or flank or even his throat, making a big ugly wound. Then, if we couldn't stop the bleeding or get a veterinarian to come soon enough, the lamb might bleed to death.

I also knew that sometimes in our territory sheep had actually been killed by dogs, especially at night. Some farmers had lost a lot of sheep that way. Once a dog had been proved guilty, and he had been shot.

But Alexander couldn't be stopped. He kept on running toward that innocent little lamb, which, for some reason, stumbled over itself, and down it went. A second later, Wally's dog crashed into him headfirst. Because Alexander had been running so fast, he lost his own balance and went into a double flip-flop, rolling over a couple of times before finally landing on his feet all ready for more action.

I don't know what happened in that dog's mind—if he had a mind—while he was turning that flip-flop and rolling over. Maybe he was so surprised that he forgot what he was doing, or maybe all of our screams upset his plans, or maybe he didn't know what he was doing in the first place. The next thing I knew, he had left the lamb and was galloping back toward us.

I could hardly believe my eyes when I saw what I saw. That little lamb, which, when it had started to run, had had a cute little dangling tail, didn't have it now, and Alexander the Coppersmith did. Alexander was galloping toward us with the lamb's tail in his mouth—a happy expression on his face, as if he had just had the best time of his life, had done something wonderful, and wanted us to think so, too.

That expression! *Honestly!* it seemed to say. *See what I did for you? I'm a wonderful dog!*

He had gone out into that pasture with only one tail and had come back with two—one on each end of him. One was fastened to him and was his own, and the other belonged to the lamb.

Well, all the gang knew what had happened. Alexander had caught hold of the lamb's tail, which, four weeks ago, had had an elastrator used on it. It had been about ready to fall off anyway. The minute he had gotten it between his teeth and given it a tug, it had come off in his mouth.

With all of us yelling at him to come back, and he probably thinking we were cheering for him, he got mixed up in his mind. The tail in his mouth was about the size of the stick he was used to carrying back to Wally, and he forgot the lamb and came back to where we were.

But Wally didn't know about a farmer using an elastrator to dock his lambs. When he saw that lamb's tail in Alexander's mouth, he got a scared expression on his face.

All the gang must have thought of the same thing at the same time, because right away we started telling him about sheep-killing dogs and how the owner of that kind of dog had to pay for any killed or badly hurt sheep.

"Sometimes the dog that is guilty has to be killed," Dragonfly said to Wally.

Well, Wally got his dog back on the leash, and we all walked along the fencerow toward the other end of the pasture where the orchard was. The gang had fun making Wally think he might be in some real trouble. He thought he might have to pay all of his one hundred dollars because of his dog's biting off the lamb's tail. A little later, though, when he began to be really worried, we stopped teasing him and told him the truth.

Not long after that, we reached the orchard —on our own side of the fence, of course— being especially careful to keep Alexander the Coppersmith on his leash. At any minute he might take a notion to jump the fence and try his success on one of the cows to see if he could come galloping back with a cow's tail in his mouth.

We couldn't let him risk it. That fierce old bull, which I was looking at right that minute, would probably make a furious headfirst rush straight for the dog and toss him back over the fence with a horn hole clear through him.

We didn't stay there very long, because we could see that Old Man Paddler was right. That was the fiercest-looking bull I had ever seen. The very minute he spied Poetry's red shirt, he turned his head toward us and stared and stared and glared and began edging toward the fence where we were, as though he would be tickled to death to show us how he could protect every one of the fifteen or more milk cows that were with him.

The cattle were all standing by the gate. It had been repaired, but I could see that if the bull wanted to, he could have torn it down in a minute—as easy as Charlotte Ann could knock down a house of blocks—and come on through it into the orchard.

We watched the cows swishing their tails

and lifting their feet nervously to keep the flies away, and then we went on, eating the apples we had in our pockets.

Alexander was the only one who didn't seem satisfied. He kept whining and straining on the end of his leash in the direction of the bull, as if he would like to show us what he could really do if he had a chance. I didn't know then that he would really get a chance before Wally's week was over.

Well, we decided it was time to go on toward home, because in an hour or so it would be time to help our folks with the chores. But Wally had never seen the Sugar Creek swamp, and we thought there would be time enough to go a little out of the way and take him through it. And that's where Alexander had another adventure.

The swamp is always a very interesting place in the summer. About halfway through it there is a big pond made by the water of Sugar Creek backing into it the way it also does about a mile farther up the creek in what we call the bayou.

We'd had many very exciting experiences in that old swamp. On the way we told Wally about different adventures we'd had there, such as the time we saw a man's head lying out in the middle of the swamp, and of the time Dragonfly saw a big black bear wallowing in the mud like a hog in a muddy barnyard, and a lot of other things that a city boy hardly ever has happen to him.

There was one place on the shore of the pond where there was a little grassy hillock, and we used to stop there and rest and watch the different things that lived in the swamp, such as dragonflies sailing around like tiny airplanes that could stop anywhere they wanted to, land on anything they wanted to, and take off again without ever having a smashup. Nearly always, a big water moccasin would be hanging from the limb of the willow that extended out over the water. And usually there would be a wild duck or two or a mud hen, swimming along, making long V-shaped water trails as they swam across from one side or one end of the pond to the other. Or a muskrat would be doing the same thing, his roundish brown head looking so friendly and his two hind feet dangling along behind him as he swam.

We kept Alexander on his leash while we went through, so that he wouldn't get off the path and wade out into the quagmire and sink in and never come back up, the way old John Till almost did once and would have if we hadn't rescued him.

We stopped right where that had happened and told Wally the whole story while Alexander whimpered and strained at his leash and tried to get away and get at everything he saw moving on the ground, swimming in the water, or climbing or flying in the trees.

"Look!" Circus exclaimed. "There's a big snapping turtle!"

I looked where Circus's forefinger and Alexander's nose were pointing. Right out in the lazy swamp water, about twenty yards from shore, I saw a shadow moving under the surface. Then the water parted, and the snapper himself came up for air, first his nose, a pair of heavy eyelids, and reddish eyes that looked like two drops of transparent blood. Then up came his wrinkled face and ugly thick neck. I got just a glimpse of the rest of him under the water and gasped. It was the biggest snapping turtle I had ever seen.

"And look!" Little Jim said beside me. "There's a mud hen."

A mud hen is the same as a marsh hen. People also call it a coot. It is a stupid bird that can't fly very fast, and hunters don't call it a game bird as they do actual ducks—mud hens are only ducklike. But they are always fun to watch. You could never tell, when they ducked themselves under, where they would come up next.

The mud hen was swimming lazily along, ducking her head under every few seconds. Then she must have seen something down in the water that she wanted. Quick as a splash, she upended herself, and down she went headfirst and tail last, going completely under, leaving only a little excited circle of water where she had been, with its waves widening out and out in every direction.

"I wish I was a mud hen," Little Jim said. But a few seconds later, he wouldn't have wanted to be.

"*Sh!*" Big Jim ordered. "Let's keep still."

And we did. Even Alexander the Coppersmith didn't move but only trembled with excitement, whimpering to get into some action of any kind, just so he wouldn't have to be still.

Then, unexpectedly, things did start to happen, and Alexander the Coppersmith got into the middle of a brand-new kind of excitement. I saw it all with my own eyes and heard it with my own ears and felt it with every nerve in my body and every cold chill that ran up and down my spine and every hair on my head that tried to stand up under my straw hat.

That mud hen, not knowing we were hiding there behind a swamp rosebush, had surfaced close to where a minute ago I had seen the big, vicious-looking, hungry-looking, bloody-eyed mud turtle. I saw her at the same time I saw the turtle's nose.

The turtle went down like a submarine, and I *knew* what was going to happen! That wrinkle-necked, powerful-jawed animal was going to sneak up under the mud hen, grab her by her pretty little webbed feet with his keen-edged cutting mandibles, and drag her down to the muddy bottom, and that would be the end of her!

I felt myself wanting to scream bloody murder and do something to save the hen. Yet I knew I couldn't.

Then, without knowing what I was going to do until I had done it, I quick stooped down, picked up a short stout stick, and threw it straight at the mud hen, yelling at the same time, "Quick! Scram! Fly! Get out of the way, or you'll be killed!" That ugly armor-plated beast wasn't going to have that cute little innocent coot for his afternoon lunch if I could help it.

Quick as a flash, my stick was on the way out across the shallow water of the pond, straight for the mud hen. It struck the water with a splash six inches from her, and down she went *ker-splash,* leaving only my stick floating in the nervous water where she had been.

Then things really began to happen on the shore.

My stout stick was Alexander the Coppersmith's invitation to do something himself. Like a flash *he* was gone, straight as a copper bullet down the bank toward the edge of the pond. He got to the end of his leash so fast that it took Wally by surprise and jerked him off his feet and into the water.

But Alexander didn't know or care what happened to Wally. He was after the stick I had thrown. It took him only seconds to swim out to get it, get it in his happy mouth, and start swimming back toward us, right past the place where I had last seen the turtle.

Well, snapping turtles are carnivorous. They eat flesh and nothing but flesh, and they don't care what kind—chicken, fish, muskrat, marsh hen, or dog. And they always eat their food underwater, not being able to swallow anything unless they have it beneath the water.

A second later, there was a terrific splashing out where Alexander was and what sounded like a hundred wild yelps of terror. Alexander dropped his stick and started thrashing around like a huge fish on a boy's line trying to get away. Then he went under, and there was only a fierce boiling of the water where he had been.

Well, there we were, six country boys on the shore of the pond in the middle of the swamp and one city boy in the shallow water near the shore. And far out in the pond, an excited city dog was under the water somewhere, battling for his life against a fierce underwater monster that was hungry for dog meat.

The dappled sunlight on the pond, made by the sun shining through the leaves of the big sycamore tree, was still a pretty sight. Only a little while before, the whole place had been alive with trilling frogs and the musical notes of red-winged blackbirds, which, along with all the other happy noises, had made the swamp sound like a big out-of-doors orchestra playing just for us. But now the music was stopped.

The whole gang came to life. Wally started screaming, "Where's Alexander the Coppersmith?" Dragonfly got allergic to the water Wally splashed on his bare feet, and he sneezed three times in quick succession. Circus, who had more presence of mind than any of the rest of us right that second, half jumped and half skidded down the slippery bank on the way to grab Wally, who was yelling, "He's gone down! He'll drown!"

Before anybody could even begin to stop Wally, he had started out into the water to where Alexander had last been seen. That really brought Circus to life. He plunged in after Wally, caught him by the shirttail, and started to drag him back.

Well, I don't know what went on under the surface of that pond or how fierce a fight was going on between a hungry turtle who was trying to keep from losing a live afternoon lunch and a dog that was trying to keep from losing his life.

But while Wally was half crying and struggling to get away from Circus so that he could save his dog, all of a sudden there was more splashing out there, and Alexander came shooting up through the surface into the sunlight. A moment later he was swimming toward the shore where we were, leaving the stick floating behind him on the nervous water, Alexander not remembering what he had gone out there for in the first place.

We were *really* having excitement! As much as I hadn't wanted Wally to come to Sugar Creek, I thought for a second that if he hadn't come we wouldn't have had all these interesting experiences, which were certainly different from any we had had before in all our lives.

And then Wally was back on shore. He and Alexander got there about the same time, both of them all wet and shaking. Wally was shaking because he was probably worried and scared, and Alexander was shaking because he was a dog and dogs always do that when they come out of the water.

Then for a minute that proud dog acted very humble. He made a wet beeline for Wally, like a very small boy hurries to his mother for comfort when he has hurt himself by stubbing his toe or bumping his nose.

And for a minute Wally was one of the happiest boys I ever saw. He dropped down on his knees and hugged Alexander around his wet neck and crooned to him as though he thought he was the best dog in the world.

And Alexander liked it and acted as if he was saying to Wally, "Poor little scared boy, did you get hurt, too? Well, don't you worry. I'll protect you." And he licked Wally's freckled face with his long tongue, which broke up their little love talk right away—Wally not liking to be kissed by a dog.

I stooped down and gave Alexander a quick examination to see how many wounds he had received in his battle with that fierce underwater quadruped.

But he wasn't badly hurt at all. He did have a one-inch-long slash just above the elbow of his right hind leg, where the snapper had probably grabbed him first. Also, the tip of one of Alexander's toes on his other foot was missing. He let me examine him without trying to jump all over me with excitement, the way he usually does.

Because not a one of us had any first-aid material with us, we decided we had better go home. Alexander's leg had to be sewed up so that it could heal better and faster.

It took us all the way home to finish talking about what had happened. By the time Wally and I got to our mailbox, the big snapping turtle was twice as big as it had been, Wally would have drowned in the shallow water if Circus hadn't jumped in and rescued him, and we had saved the life of a beautiful wild duck by scaring it away from the open jaws of the huge snapping turtle. Anyway, that's how Wally stretched the story to Mom and Dad. I helped him a little by keeping still—sort of hating to interrupt him when the turtle, which he hadn't seen at all but I had, got bigger and bigger as he talked.

It took my dad only a few minutes to give Alexander first aid. He had a lot of first-aid equipment such as a special needle and thread and antiseptics, which he kept in the cupboard in the barn to use on our horses and cows when they got hurt. It was as easy as pie for him to take care of a dog that had had a fight underwater with a vicious, web-footed, flesh-eating, half-as-big-as-a-bull snapping turtle!

9

The days dragged past, and my little black and white polecat alarm clock ticked off the minutes for me as fast as it could, day and night. There were a lot of things Wally and I actually had fun doing, such as stalking bullfrogs with a lantern at night, catching a lot of them and having fried frogs' legs for breakfast next morning, and catching pigeons in the haymow of Little Jim's dad's barn and selling them to a poultry man in town. Wally saved his share of the money to put in the bank when he got home.

We got our "red lips redder still, kissed by strawberries on the hill." We went swimming at least once a day so we wouldn't have to take so many baths. Also we went fishing for chubs in the riffles and for sunfish and goggle-eyes near the mouth of the branch. Sometimes at night my dad went fishing with us, and we caught catfish down by the Sugar Creek bridge.

Nearly always when we went fishing at night, we left Alexander at home, tied to the grape-arbor post, so he wouldn't scare the fish away.

Several times we went past Old Man Paddler's orchard to see if it would be safe to get any apples, and it always wasn't. When Alexander was with us, he acted as if he was still disappointed we didn't let him have a fight with the bull the first time we were there. "After all," his face seemed to say, "didn't I half kill a savage mud turtle that was almost as big as a bull?"

His leg wound healed fast, and he didn't seem to mind having the tip of one toe missing. I expected him to calm down a little as the minutes dragged along, because I thought maybe in the city he hadn't had enough exercise and he was just running wild in the country to work off all his nervous energy. But I must have been wrong, because he kept right on being as excitable as ever, day and night—the nights getting worse as the week got nearer to Sunday. I had managed to teach him a few lessons, but only a few.

Then one night he ran into trouble for sure with nearly three thousand minutes left, and I was getting to be almost as nervous as he was.

Some of his trouble was because of his curiosity, which was worse than a cat's. He still ate his no-odor dog biscuits three times a day, and naturally he wasn't supposed to smell like a dog, which naturally he did. And those dog biscuits didn't keep him from using his long cold nose to smell everything under the Sugar Creek sun, in order to find out what it was and why.

Dad tried to defend him to me by saying, "How else can he learn what a thing is, if he can't smell it? That's the way dogs figure things out—with their noses."

"You mean they have their brains in their noses?" I asked. And because Dad didn't laugh, maybe that wasn't very funny.

He and I were out by the grape arbor at the time, watching that wriggling copper-colored quadruped sniffing and zigzagging his way along the garden fence.

"I hope he doesn't take a notion to jump over the fence into the garden," I said, which, right that second, Alexander did. Up and over he went, before you could have said "Jack Robinson Crusoe."

Wally himself was in the house at the time. He and Mom were visiting together about something. That was another thing I couldn't understand. For some reason, my mother had seemed to take a fancy to Wally, and nearly every one of the four or five days he had been here, he had gone into the house while she was making a pie or something. He would sit on the wooden bench behind the table and eat cookies, and they would talk and talk—about what, I didn't know. They always stopped when I came in, and right away Wally would shove the last of his cooky into his mouth and be ready to go somewhere to do or see something.

Well, Alexander hadn't any sooner landed in the garden, probably on two or three of Mom's cabbage plants, than she came to the door to call Dad to the telephone.

"Who is it?" he asked, as he always does.

Mom answered, "I don't know. Some man. He sounded a little impatient."

Dad started toward the house, and then turned around to me and said, "Run on out to the garden and explain to Alexander that gardens are not for dogs to play in. And show him the gate."

I was glad to do it. I not only showed him the gate, but I went into the garden and explained to him in no uncertain terms that he was not to jump the fence again, not ever.

That was another thing. So far, there wasn't a fence around the farm or up and down the creek or anywhere that could keep the animal out. He would either go through it or under it or over it.

By using a very friendly voice, I managed to coax him out of the garden and up to the grape arbor where his leash was.

In spite of my not liking him very much at first, I'd felt sorry for him ever since he'd gotten the tip of his toe snapped off. Once or twice I had a feeling that he and I could become friends, but he didn't seem to be interested. It was just as if he had had a hard enough time learning to like one freckle-faced boy and couldn't stand the thought of taking the trouble to learn to like another.

If only he wouldn't keep on acting as if he owned the place—not only our farm but the whole neighborhood! What right had a dog to act like that anyway? The only actual owner of the woods and the trees and everything in his neighborhood is the boy who lives there, who likes them better than almost anything in the world, and who uses them for his playground without tearing them all to pieces with his teeth and scaring the living daylights out of everything that is alive.

Like the rest of the Sugar Creek Gang, I had always sort of felt that all the birds' nests and the tiny, fuzzy baby birds that were hatched in them and all the cute little rabbits that hippety-hopped around the farm and all the walnut-eating, walnut-burying, tree-climbing, bushy-tailed squirrels and all the fish in Sugar Creek and the wildflowers and everything were all mine. Even the big lazy white clouds that sailed across the sky like ships up where the fork-tailed, black-throated barn swallows darted swiftly around catching insects—*everything* belonged to me.

So naturally I resented having a dog move into the neighborhood and take over, even if only for ten thousand eighty minutes.

Alexander even acted as if he owned the caterpillars, and that they hadn't any right to live. Just one hour ago, when I'd been sitting on the board platform beside the iron pitcher pump, watching a fuzzy red-brown and black caterpillar as it crawled innocently along, and wondering what kind of butterfly or moth it would someday become, Alexander, who had been fooling around by the walnut tree and the mailbox, got tired of what he was doing and came nosing up to where I was to see if I was having any fun he was missing out on. He stopped about three feet from me.

"Come here a minute, old pal," I said. "You're a nice doggie. Come on."

Well, he came. For a small minute he let me put my hand on his withers, which is the back of a dog's neck, and he acted as if he was fascinated with the caterpillar, too.

"Look," I said to him, "see that cute little fuzzy caterpillar? Well, one of these days it will get tired of being just a worm crawling around on the ground and on people's board walks and will wrap itself up in a cocoon. Then, after it has slept awhile, maybe through the winter, it will come out. And when it does, it won't be a caterpillar anymore. It will be a pretty butterfly of some kind and will fly all round over the neighborhood. Now, don't you think that's nice?" And I patted Alexander on his poll, which is the top of his head.

For a minute longer he let me hug him. I began to explain to him that there was a very wonderful God up in heaven and also everywhere, who had made all the things in nature, even dogs.

But Alexander didn't care who made him. All of a sudden, when the caterpillar started crawling in his direction, he got a gruff growl in his throat. Then his right front paw shot out and scratched at it. And that was the last of his lesson in nature and also the last of the caterpillar, which was supposed to be the second stage of a butterfly. It was squished into a little blob of yellowish and greenish jelly on the pump platform.

One other lesson I had tried hard to teach him was not to bark at night. I had tried it last night, in fact, and for the first time he had seemed to understand what being quiet meant. I had learned how to do it from the book I'd gotten myself all wet for.

About midnight, as usual, he started barking at the moon or something else he saw or smelled, or thought he saw or smelled, and he wouldn't stop. Wally wakened and came stumbling into my room to scold him through the screened window. I also scolded him, but he still kept on barking.

Then I remembered the book and said to Wally, "I'll go down and ask him to please let us sleep."

Wally, being used to Alexander's barking, went back to bed.

I pushed my feet into my slippers and felt my way down the dark, long room under my dad's seed corn, around the corner of the banister, and down the stairs.

Pretty soon, I was outdoors in the moonlight beside Alexander, saying to him in my kindest voice, "What's the matter, pal? Nervous? That's too bad. Now, don't you be scared. That old man in the moon is as kind as Old Man Paddler."

That's what the book said—a dog that barks at night is a nervous dog and needs to be reassured. So I used my reassuring voice on him, and he let me come up to him and pet him.

I kept on crooning to him, stooped low and hugged him and said, "You're an awful nice doggie, *awful* nice. But don't you know there are human beings in the house behind me who have to get up early in the morning and work hard all day? And we have to have some sleep."

He seemed to appreciate my getting up out of a cozy bed with clean sheets on it to hug a dog that slept on a no-odor cedar-treated mattress. He gave his cold nose a quick turn, touched my face with it, and a second later his long tongue licked me on the cheek, as much as to say, "I guess I can stand another freckle-faced boy after all." And in that very second I thought I liked him pretty well.

Then I noticed that his leather collar was awfully tight, and I remembered that every time my dad lay down anywhere in the daytime to take a snooze, he would unbutton the top button of his shirt to let his throat relax. He could breathe better, he said.

"Poor little dog," I comforted Alexander, "your collar is too tight. No wonder you can't sleep." So I loosened the collar just one notch, patted him on his poll again, told him again what a wonderful dog he was, and coaxed him to lie down on his cedar-treated mattress, which he did. Then I went back into the house and upstairs to bed. I took a look at my alarm clock and noticed it was about five minutes after twelve, which meant I still could get a lot of good sleep.

But it seemed I hadn't any sooner dropped

off to sleep than I was awakened again by Alexander's barking. I was disgusted. I didn't want to wake up. Even worse, I didn't want to get up, but I knew that, with a dog barking outside my window, I would be awakened all the rest of the night, over and over and over again, and be a wreck in the morning and feel grumpy all day.

I looked at my clock once more and was surprised to notice it was three o'clock already. Alexander had been quiet three whole hours. But, "Bark, bark, bark, bark, bark, bark, bark!" Alexander the Coppersmith was all nervous again.

I dragged myself out of bed and fumbled my way down the room to the banister and downstairs again, through the kitchen and out into the moonlight, hardly noticing that it was one of the prettiest moonlit nights I'd ever seen or smelled. The new-mown hay in Dragonfly's dad's hayfield smelled like a million dollars.

But when I got out on the board walk and started toward the cedar-treated mattress, I saw that Alexander the Coppersmith wasn't there. I knew right away what had happened. He had been so nervous that he had pulled and tugged and worried his head out of his loosened collar.

He was out by the plum tree, barking in the direction of Old Man Paddler's pasture. He probably smelled the cattle or maybe the sheep, and it was hard for him to sleep with an odor like that, especially when he wasn't used to it.

As mad as I was for having to wake up, I still wanted to prove to myself that I was a good dog trainer. So I coaxed him back to his bed, talked nicely to him, and in a few minutes had him calmed down so that he wasn't trembling.

"Now," I said to him, "you stay here. And just for slipping your collar, you have to have it tight the rest of the night."

He licked my hand and, before I could get away, my face also.

After crooning over him a little longer, I stroked his withers and patted his poll and stumbled my still sleepy way back up the stairs to my room, where I went to sleep on Mom's clean pillowcase without washing my dog-kissed face.

The next thing I knew it was a bright sun-shiny morning with a whole day ahead of me to have fun in and also probably to work in. I looked out the window at Alexander. He was still there, standing up in his bed and barking again at something or other. But it was all right then, because it was time for all of us to be awake anyway.

I certainly felt proud of myself for being such a good dog trainer and helping Alexander —and all the rest of us—to get a lot of needed sleep. All except Wally, who didn't need any help.

Being kind to Alexander had worked twice last night, and it also had worked this morning. While Dad was in the house answering the phone, I had talked Alexander out of the gar-

den and all the way across the barnyard to the
grape arbor. I was just snapping the leash onto
his tight enough collar when Dad came out the
back door to where I was.

I noticed he had a kind of worried expression on his face.

"Who was it?" I said.

"Harm Groenwald," he said. "The cattleman who rented Old Man Paddler's pasture."

"What did he want?" I asked.

And Dad answered, "He's all burned up
about something. He's got two dead lambs this
morning. Somebody's dogs—or dog—got into
the pasture last night and killed them." He
sighed and then finished, "But I told him our
dog couldn't possibly have done it, because he
was tied right here all night."

When my dad said that, I got a sick sensation in the pit of my stomach. Like a terribly
fast-moving story, I was remembering that
Alexander had chased sheep and pulled off a
lamb's tail in that same pasture earlier in the
week. Also I was remembering that at three
o'clock in the morning he had been loose—
and maybe had been for three whole hours.

I was so weak for a minute that you could
have knocked me over with a small whirlwind.
A terribly fast whirlwind was going round in my
mind right that minute, scattering my thoughts
all over the Sugar Creek territory. I certainly
wouldn't put it past that dog to chase sheep or
anything else at midnight.

Just then Wally came out to see what we

were doing and why. Something in my mind said I had better tell my dad about what happened last night, but with Wally there, I hated to say it and have him think my dog training venture had been such a failure.

10

I tell you it doesn't feel very good to have
something on your mind like I had on mine,
knowing that Alexander had been loose part of
last night—probably long enough to have
killed two innocent lambs in Harm Groenwald's pasture. If it could be proved that
Wally's dog had actually done it, Wally would
have to pay for the loss of both of them—probably twenty-five dollars apiece.

It had been fun teasing Wally about it when
Alexander had come galloping back with a
lamb's tail in his mouth, but now it was different. Why, Alexander himself might even have
to be killed.

Then I got an idea. If Alexander *had* actually killed those two lambs, there might be traces
of blood in his mouth. There might even be
bits of wool caught between his teeth, the way a
boy gets bits of fried chicken in his when he
eats. He might have gotten so hungry, being
tired of no-odor dog biscuits, that he had killed
the lambs on purpose to get a taste of fresh
mutton.

I coaxed him to let me look at his teeth.

Alexander didn't like the idea very well,
and Wally, who was watching, said, "What are
you trying to do to him?"

"Nothing," I said, "I'm just examining his teeth."

"They're all right," Wally assured me. "I took him to a dentist just before we left Memory City."

"The *dentist!*" I had never heard of such a thing as taking a dog to a dentist.

Well, the day was started, and we had a lot of things to do before another one thousand forty minutes would be gone. Then there would be another day, and after that, Sunday, when Wally would go to Sunday school and church with us. It would probably be his first time to go in a long time because Uncle Amos and my red aunt had quit going, which meant that Wally had been growing up to be an American heathen.

Believe me, we kept Alexander tied up every night. I was especially careful to see to it that he was and also that his collar was good and tight. As the nights passed, and nobody's dogs or dog bothered Mr. Groenwald's or anybody else's sheep, I kept wondering if Alexander really had killed the two lambs between midnight and three o'clock on the one night he had been loose.

I knew that before long—certainly before Wally left—I'd have to tell somebody about it, because if Harm Groenwald's sheep had been raided on only that one night, then Alexander must have been the guilty dog. I still didn't want to tell Wally, because he'd think I was a failure as a dog trainer, and he might blame me for the dead lambs. Also, he'd worry because he'd be afraid Alexander might have to be shot. I didn't like to tell Dad because—well, because I just didn't. And if I told Mom, she might get hurt in her heart, and that'd make mine hurt even worse. It seemed there wasn't anybody I could tell.

And as my little polecat clock kept ticking off the minutes, I kept feeling sadder and sadder. *Of course,* I thought, *I could keep still till after Uncle Amos and my red aunt come back from their vacation, and then both Wally and Alexander will be gone, and everything will be all right—or will it?*

Then Sunday morning came, and we all went to Sunday school and church, where I got the surprise of my life. Wally, who was in the same class with the rest of the gang, knew the answer to practically every question our teacher asked.

I couldn't believe my ears. *What on earth?* I thought. I simply couldn't understand how a boy who hardly ever went to Sunday school and didn't know beans about the Bible could, all of a sudden, know practically everything about that rather hard lesson.

During the church service, which followed Sunday school, I learned something that made me feel even worse about Mr. Groenwald's two dead lambs and Alexander the Coppersmith and Wally. Sylvia's dad's sermon—the part of it that was especially for boys and girls—was a true story about Robert Louis Stevenson. As nearly everybody knows, he was a famous writer who lived a long time ago and who wrote a lot of books, such as *Treasure Island* and a book of poems called *A Child's Garden of Verses.*

When Sylvia's dad mentioned *A Child's Garden of Verses,* I looked at Poetry to see if he was listening. He was, with both hands up to his ears. That reminded me of the way Alexander looked when *he* listened to something, with both of his copper ears standing straight up and with his nose pointing in the direction the sound was coming from.

For a second I imagined myself to be a dog listening with my ears straight up. Then, because I felt myself smiling at myself for being a dog, I frowned instead, because anybody, especially my parents, wouldn't understand why I was smiling and would think I shouldn't.

Well, when Robert Louis Stevenson was just a little guy, he had a nurse taking care of him, as small boys did in those days in his country, which was Scotland. First, Sylvia's dad quoted part of a poem that Robert Louis Stevenson once wrote and which goes like this:

> In winter I get up at night
> And dress by yellow candle light;
> In summer, quite the other way,
> I have to go to bed by day.

Poor little Robert Louis Stevenson, I thought and felt sorry for him. It had been so long since I was little and had to go to bed by day that I could hardly remember it. But in the winter I still had to get up before daylight to get breakfast over and the chores done and started off to our one room, red brick school, to get there on time. I had memorized that little poem myself when I was in the second grade.

Sylvia's dad went on to tell us that one day when it was time for little Robert to go to bed, he didn't want to go. He wanted to stay outdoors until it got dark. It was *almost* dark but not quite, and he was sitting out on the steps looking up at the stars. His nurse called him to come in three times, and still he didn't come. So she went out to get him.

"What are you doing out here? Why didn't you come when I called you?" she asked.

Little Robert answered, "I'm out here watching God open up lights in the darkness," meaning he was watching God turn on the stars one at a time.

Then Sylvia's dad explained that every Christian ought to do more than just watch God turn on lights in people's hearts—we ought to help Him do it. "Have you turned on the light in anybody's heart this week?" he asked.

I couldn't think of anybody I had done that to. I had been trying to turn on a few lights in a dog's mind. But so far, Alexander had turned most of them off again.

When we got home and Dad and I were out by the garden waiting for dinner to be ready, I told him about Wally being able to answer practically every question the teacher asked.

Dad said, "You can give your mother credit for that. She spent all week opening up lights in his mind."

"She *what?*" I asked.

So Dad explained that at the beginning of the week Wally had told Mom he didn't want to go to Sunday school because he didn't want to seem like a dumbbell in class. So she had taught him the lesson ahead of time—which explains what he and Mom were doing nearly every day while she baked pies or cakes and did other things in the kitchen. And he helped her by sitting on the bench behind the table, listening—and also eating cookies, which was the way Mom got him to sit still long enough for her to turn the lights on, since his mind was a pretty dark place.

Then Dad and I went in to dinner.

But I didn't feel very good. It seemed God was trying to turn on a light somewhere, and He wanted me to help Him do it. I kept thinking about it all through dinner, not eating as much as I usually do, and I excused myself before the rest of the family and Wally were done.

I went outdoors to Alexander's cedar-treated mattress, where he had just finished his dinner of no-odor dog biscuits. He was standing up in his bed, looking hungrily at the kitchen door and probably smelling our fried chicken and wishing he could have some.

I stooped down and hugged him. "Listen, little dog friend," I said to him, "I know all about what you did last Wednesday night. But it's all my fault. I'm to blame. I didn't do it on purpose but was only trying to turn on a light in your mind. And now Wally, or I, or somebody, owes Harm Groenwald about fifty dollars, and maybe you'll have to be shot to death."

He touched my cheek with his cold nervous nose and, before I could get away, licked my face with his long red tongue.

Then I got another idea. I moseyed on out to the barn and went inside and climbed the ladder to the alfalfa-smelling haymow. That was where I used to keep my little New Testament in a crack in a log away up on top of a hill of hay near the roof. I used to kneel down there in the hay and tell the One who made the stars practically all the troubles I ever had. And nearly always He would take them away or make me think of something I could do to get rid of them myself.

"Hi, old Bentcomb," I said to my favorite hen.

She was sitting on her favorite nest, waiting till she could get her daily egg laid and then get out with the rest of the hens in the barnyard. She didn't answer but sort of ducked her head, as much as to say, "Don't bother me. I'm busy."

Then I went on up to my corner.

Even before I started to pray, it seemed I knew what I was supposed to do. I had one hundred dollars in the bank, I thought, and would still have fifty dollars left if I went to Mr. Groenwald and gave him twenty-five for each dead lamb. Also, if I took Alexander with me and let him see what a fine dog he was, what a pretty half-long nose he had, how active he was, how he would sit up and bark for a biscuit you offered him and would chase after a stick and bring it galloping back to you, and how he had learned not to bark at night (not as bad as he used to, anyway), and explain how he was a city dog and not used to country life and didn't know any better—then maybe Mr. Groenwald would like Alexander and forgive him and everything would be all right.

I wouldn't even need to tell Mom or Dad or Wally or anybody at all, although I supposed Dad would find out about my taking fifty dollars from my savings account and want to know why. But I wouldn't mind telling him after Wally's ten thousand minutes were over and he was gone.

When I got through praying, I stood up, for a minute looking down at the place where my two knees had been. I felt very happy inside, as if I had maybe done one of the most important things in the world.

Of course, my prayer hadn't sounded much like Old Man Paddler's had, but it did seem I had been talking to the same wonderful Person he had. And it didn't make any difference where anybody was when he talked to Him—in an old Abraham Lincoln style cabin in the hills, or in the moonlight that filtered in through a boy's bedroom window, or on a hill of alfalfa hay in the haymow of a Sugar Creek barn. He was always glad to listen.

Then I climbed down the haymow ladder and went outdoors again. Old Mixy spied me and started meowing toward me, and I knew that she was in a hurry to rub her innocent sides against my pant legs. Her tail was straight up in the air, the way it always is when she walks like that. It was just like the tail of the little black and white animal out in the woods, except that her tail didn't mean the same thing because she wasn't that kind of a kitty.

She followed all around me till she got almost to the grape arbor. There she stopped stock-still and spit, arching her back at the same time toward Alexander, who growled back at her from the end of his tight leash. Then she decided to go on back to the barn and did.

I stopped beside Alexander, who, as soon as he stopped looking at Mixy, pushed a friendly nose into my hand as if we were good friends.

"Well, old pal," I said, "it's all set. The first chance we get, we're going to take a walk through the woods, just the two of us."

11

Now that it was all settled in my mind what I had to do, I realized that I had to get going on it as quick as I could or it would be too late.

While I was still talking to Alexander, Dad called me from the back door, saying, "Bill, telephone!"

I quickly went into the house, passing the stack of dishes in the kitchen sink with a sinking sensation in my mind and went on into the front room to the telephone.

It was Poetry, wanting to know if Wally and I could come over to his house and sleep in his big tent that night. "We'll have to get going, or it will be too late."

"Get going on what?" I asked.

He answered, "Don't you remember? We were going to take Wally to our hideout in the toolshed loft."

I had been hoping maybe Poetry would forget about that. The mischievous things he and I had planned to do to Wally had seemed wonderful before Wally had come, when I still thought he was dumber than any boy I had ever seen. But after what happened that morning during the Sunday school lesson, he didn't seem like such a scatterbrained boy after all.

Also, right that minute I wasn't in a mischievous mood, because of Alexander and the two dead lambs. So I said to Poetry, "Wait a minute. I'll ask Mom," hoping she would say no, as she had done quite a few times in my life when I had wanted to stay all night with Poetry in his big tent.

I laid the phone on the lamp pedestal of our old-fashioned organ and went out to the kitchen.

"Poetry wants Wally and me to sleep in his big tent tonight. You don't want us to, do you?" I looked at Mom's face, which I had never gotten tired of looking at, even if it wasn't as pretty as my red aunt's or Little Jim's mom's. Little Jim's mom was the prettiest mother in the whole Sugar Creek territory.

But Mom didn't say no. "Yes," she said. "I think that will be all right. What do you say, Wally?"

"It's all right with me," Wally said. "Sure, I'd like that."

And that was the beginning of what was going to make our little whirlwind, which had started when Wally came, turn into a tornado.

Wally and I decided to go over to Poetry's in the afternoon to take our pajamas and also Alexander the Coppersmith's mattress and a package of no-odor biscuits. Wally insisted that Alexander had to sleep there, too. "He'd be too nervous sleeping here all alone, and he might bark all night and keep your folks awake," he said.

So we loaded everything in my little red coaster wagon, which I used to play with a lot when I was little and which I still used to pull Charlotte Ann around in.

"What you taking the alarm clock for?" Wally asked when he and I started out toward the walnut tree.

Before I thought, I said, "That's to tell us when it's midnight."

"Midnight! Who wants to know when it's midnight when he's asleep?"

I managed to change the subject, because it was at midnight that Poetry and I planned to wake Wally and take him on a little walk to Poetry's dad's log cabin, which had a family of black and white woods cats living under it.

I still didn't know how we were going to get Wally to go with us, but Poetry had told me on the phone that it was his secret and to quit worrying about how. "Just trust me," he had said.

At the last moment, Mom decided to send along some old sheets for our cots, so Poetry's mom wouldn't have to furnish her own. Poetry's mother would think that was nice of Mom, I thought.

Since both families were going to church at night, as nearly all the Sugar Creek Gang's parents did every Sunday, we could have our cots made up and be ready to tumble into them the minute we got home to Poetry's house.

As we rambled along down the road, pulling the little red wagon behind us, I was wishing all the time that Poetry would change his mind.

It didn't take us long to get to the little lane that leads past the toolshed. Wally was pulling the wagon at the time, and Alexander was pulling me. He was on the dog end of the leash and I on the other.

"Let's go get a skunk this afternoon," Wally said.

All week long he had been teasing me to help him catch one, and every time I had talked him out of it, giving him nine reasons. Two of them were my parents, and seven of them were the mother skunk and her six kittens, every one of which, I warned Wally, carried a musk pouch and could spray six times without stopping, which would be forty-two shots a boy would have to dodge.

So when Wally said, "Let's go get a skunk," and at the same time Alexander acted as if he was in favor of it, I said flatly, *"Absolutely not!"*

"But you can sell one for twenty-five dollars," Wally argued. "Wouldn't you like twenty-five dollars?"

"It's worth twenty-five dollars not to get shot." Then I remembered and told him, "They don't generally come out until around twilight or after dark, and the only safe way to catch one without getting perfumed is like Circus did it."

Once more Wally let me talk him out of it, but I could see he had his mind on the twenty-five dollars and was willing to run the risk of getting shot with something that was a lot stronger than three parts water and one part household ammonia.

As we went on toward Poetry's tent, both he and Alexander had on their faces the same stubborn expression I had seen there before.

Well, the afternoon passed, and night came, and we all went to church and heard one of Old Man Paddler's missionaries give a very interesting talk with pictures of his work in a South American mission field. The talk was an especially good one for Wally to hear, because a missionary was as strange to him as an animal in the zoo would be to Alexander the Coppersmith. Wally had never in his life seen a real missionary, and I could tell by looking at his face that he had had another light turned on in his mind.

Finally the three of us were back at Poetry's tent getting ready for bed. Poetry and I were inside alone for a few minutes while Wally was out tying up Alexander and giving him final instructions about how to behave when he was away from home, reminding him to use his very best dog manners.

"That," I heard him say in no uncertain terms, "is the *moon*. You are not to bark at it! And that shadow over there by the edge of the garden is a clothesline post. You are not to bark at *it!* Do you understand?"

And Alexander was probably saying back to Wally in dog language, "Don't worry, I won't bark at anything till Bill Collins gets to sleep. Then I'll probably find something that'll make me very nervous, and I'll start in."

I still didn't have the slightest idea how we could talk Wally into going for a walk at midnight. So while he was still outside, I whispered to Poetry, "Let's call it off. I'm not in favor of it anyway."

"And why not?" he wanted to know. "It's our last chance—our last night."

"That's just the trouble," I said. "What if Wally or Alexander gets mixed up with a skunk? They'll have to stay another week to get the smell off them."

"Don't let that worry you. There isn't a chance in the world."

"There are six little chances and one big one," I said.

"Didn't I tell you? Mama Skunk moved her family out five days ago—clear out of the neighborhood. Circus caught another one of her kittens, and she must have gotten scared she'd lose her whole family, so she moved."

"I'm still not in favor of it," I said firmly.

"Don't you believe in majority rule?" he asked.

"Sure," I answered, "but there are only two of us, and the vote is one against one."

"How much do you weigh?"

I said, "Eighty-seven."

He said, "Then it's settled. I weigh one hundred forty-nine. So that's one hundred forty-nine to eighty-seven that we go ahead with our plans."

It was silly, but he was so enthusiastic, and so absolutely sure the idea was good, that my eighty-seven gave in to his one hundred forty-nine, and the majority ruled, even though I still didn't know how he had planned to make Wally want to go.

"Just trust me," he said.

But when you trust one hundred forty-nine pounds of a boy like Poetry, you are trusting one hundred forty-nine pounds of mischief with sixteen ounces to every pound, which is two thousand three hundred fifty-two ounces.

It took Wally only a few seconds to give his final order to Alexander and to lift the tent flap and come back inside. He looked funny crawling in. The light of Poetry's lantern made his face look like a ghost's.

I wondered what Wally would do when Poetry and I got down on our knees to say our quiet prayers before we tumbled in. But when he saw us kneeling, he got down beside his own cot and stayed there till we got up and crawled into bed. Then he did the same thing without saying a word, which made me wish harder than ever that we weren't going to be mischievous at midnight. Not that I couldn't be mischievous when I had to, or wanted to, but I was still thinking of Mr. Groenwald's lambs.

Poetry blew out the lantern then, and it was only a little while until Wally was snoring away, and so was Poetry. It was a very interesting duet with Wally snoring bass and Poetry a kind of tenor and both of their snores being a little off pitch.

I stayed awake, listening to my little polecat clock ticking away the minutes, hurrying as fast as it could toward midnight.

That was another thing. Poetry had set the clock in the bottom of the utility can that he and I had found at the dump. "It will make more noise," he had said, "and we'll be sure to wake up."

I kept on lying there in the half dark, listening to the maple leaves whispering in the branches above our tent and thinking about God again and how He liked Wally as much as He did us. I knew He wouldn't care if boys had a lot of innocent fun, because He had made us that way and we couldn't help it. But it didn't seem the right time to be mischievous. Maybe I should have told Poetry about the night Alexander had been loose and how I had planned to go over and offer Mr. Groenwald fifty dollars to pay for his two dead lambs.

I thought how easy it would be for me to reach out and shut off the alarm. Then, when midnight came, all of us would sleep right on through till morning. But as I always do at night, I got more and more sleepy, and without knowing it I dropped off and probably began snoring as loud as Poetry or Wally or both.

All of a sudden I almost jumped off my cot. I was awakened by a terrible jangling noise beside me, which was my little polecat alarm clock going off in the bottom of the utility can, where it had gone off once before when it had a black and white kitty beside it.

Such a noise! Wally, beside me on his cot, jumped awake and sat straight up. I quickly reached for the can to plunge my hand down inside and shut off the alarm. But in the dark I hit it, knocked it off the table it was on, and it landed with a *whammy-sock-bang-bang* on the ground. My arm had struck the can so hard that it rolled clear to the end of the tent where the opening was and out-of-doors, with the alarm still in there and ringing like everything.

Well, that woke up Alexander the Coppersmith, who maybe got as scared as the old wolf in the story of the wolf and the little pig, when a butter churn rolled down the hill and frightened him so badly that he ran home. I suppose if that can had been a snapping turtle or another dog or a car or a lamb or a squirrel, Alexander would have made a dive for it, but instead he made a dive *from* it.

Even if I had made up my mind I wanted to stay in my cozy cot and not get up to follow a crazy boy's idea out into the middle of a crazy adventure, I would have had to get up anyway, because right that minute I discovered that Wally had tied Alexander to one of the main poles of the tent.

There was a sudden violent shaking of the whole tent, and the next thing I knew the tent pole was yanked loose and my side of the tent came swishing down on top of where I was lying, making me disgusted and wide awake and stirring up my temper so that I was ready to fight anybody or anything.

In the middle of the confusion, I managed to scramble out into the moonlight to where Alexander was still struggling to get loose and also where my polecat clock was still alarming like mad over near the base of the maple tree, with the utility can on its side beside it.

Then Poetry's squawky voice called out beside me, "Hey, you guys! There goes something! Look! Running into the woods!"

Alexander saw it at the same time and started after it, dragging the tent pole with him.

"What is it?" I said, and so did Wally, his voice shaking. And what to my wondering eyes should appear but something tall and white galloping through the woods toward Sugar Creek.

12

When you've been sleeping soundly in a tent in your friend's yard and all of a sudden are awakened by a noisy alarm clock going off in the bottom of a can—and when you try to turn the alarm off and instead you knock over the can and it rolls outdoors with the clock in it still alarming—and before you can even start to think, your tent begins to reel and rock and stagger and shake as if a tornado has hit it, and then it falls in on your cot, and two boys and a dog turn their voices loose with a lot of excited noise—and when you manage to save your life by crawling out into the moonlit night, only to discover that there has been a ghost snooping around, and you see the ghost or whatever it is, tall and white, running or floating through the woods—well, when all *that* happens, you feel you've never been in the middle of so much excitement in your life.

Anyway, that's the way I felt as three barefoot boys in flapping pajamas, and a dog dragging a tent pole, ran *stumblety-sizzle* after a ghost in a flapping bed sheet—for that's what it seemed it was and what it had on.

"There!" Poetry yelled over his shoulder—he was ahead of the rest of us at the time. "It's making a beeline for the toolshed."

"It's g–g–g–gone inside!" Wally stuttered beside me, and sure enough it had. *Bang!* went the toolshed door, loud enough to wake up the neighborhood.

With the slamming of that door, we all stood still and shook with fear or surprise or something. I did, anyway. Even Alexander the Coppersmith stopped, which gave Wally a chance to catch hold of his leash and to untie him from the tent pole. I decided I'd carry it myself from then on—not that I was so scared I had to have something in my hands, but I thought we might want to go back to the tent to sleep the rest of the night, and we'd need the pole to hold it up.

We weren't any more than fifty feet from the toolshed. I was waiting for Poetry to do or say something or for something to happen. I knew there wasn't any such thing as a ghost, but Wally didn't know it, and neither did Alexander, who was so nervous he was trembling all over and, for a change, seemed glad to stay close to his master.

Then Wally asked in a husky whisper, "Is it a real ghost?"

"Why not?" Poetry answered in a terribly scared-sounding voice. He sounded so frightened that I thought he really was. "It's not the way I planned it," he whispered to me. The way he said it sent cold chills up and down my spine. Maybe it *was* a ghost, even if there weren't any such things in the world.

I had my eyes glued to the closed door of

the toolshed. Then I looked at the loft window just above it, and all of a sudden I saw that window move! *Move,* mind you! It was being opened!

And then I heard a piercing wail as high-pitched as a woman's high soprano and sounding like the quavering voice of a screech owl crying, *"Shay–a–a–a–a–a! Shay–a–a–a!"* followed by actual words as clear as moonlight and also absolutely crazy. The words were "I—*am*—*the* —*ghost*—*of*—*Walford*—*Sensenbrenner! I*—*am*— *Walford*—*Sensenbrenner's*—*ghost!"*

It was the wildest, weirdest cry I had heard in my life.

Then Poetry yelled a squawky yell toward the shed. "We don't care who you are. You can't fool us! There isn't any such thing as a ghost!"

The ghost, or whoever or whatever it was, started its piercing wail again, this time crying, *"I*—*am*—*the*—*ghost*—*of*—*Alexander*—*the*—*Coppersmith! I*—*am*—*Alexander*—*the*—*Coppersmith's* —*ghost. I*—*am*—*a dead dog!"* And immediately the voice changed and began barking a high-pitched excited bark so much like Alexander's bark that I had to look down to see if he was still with us. He was still trembling beside Wally but growling a deep gruff growl way down in his throat.

Again Poetry yelled up at the window. "We're coming in to get you, whoever you are! Follow me," he ordered Wally and Alexander and me and led the way toward the toolshed door.

"I'm s–s–scared," Wally said.

If I could have seen his face, it would probably have looked worse than his voice sounded, which was pretty bad. But he, Alexander, and I followed anyway to the dark door.

Poetry yanked the door open and called in a savage voice, "Come on down and out of that loft, whoever you are!"

The human voice of the ghost answered in a sobbing wail, "All right, I will. But remember I am already dead."

Unbelievably quick, there was a sound like a body being dragged across the floor up there, and a moment later something big and awkward and wrapped in a sheet fell down the ladder to the toolshed floor, rolled over, and stopped in a sprawl at our feet.

"It's the body of a man!" Wally cried, jumping backward to get out of the way. He let out a scream, and I guess I did myself.

Then I heard somebody snicker upstairs and somebody else say, *"Sh!"* And a whole chorus of voices exploded in our direction. "We're *all* ghosts! Come on up and get *all* of us."

It was the voices of the rest of the grandest gang of boys there ever was in the world—Big Jim, our leader; Dragonfly, the pop-eyed member; Circus, the monkey-faced mischief maker; and Little Jim himself. Then I knew it was only a joke. The body at our feet was just a sack of straw tied in the middle and wrapped in a sheet.

There was a flash of light in the attic and the sound of somebody lighting Poetry's lantern.

"Let's go up," Poetry said.

We did, first tying Alexander to the spoke of an old cultivator wheel, and then climbing the ladder to the loft.

"You got here just in time," Big Jim said to us. "It's a specially called gang meeting. Something very important has come up, making it necessary."

The first thing I said was "How come all your parents allowed you to come to the shed at midnight?"

Dragonfly, whose crooked nose looked more crooked in the lantern light, sniffed and said, "It's not midnight. It's only a little after ten o'clock."

"But," I said to Poetry, "my alarm was set for midnight."

"Sure it was, and it went off at midnight too, but it was two hours too fast."

"It—*what!*"

"I changed it myself one time when you weren't looking," Poetry explained.

Well, it was a wonderful way for a mystery to turn out.

Circus, who had been the ghost, was still dressed in his bedsheet. "It was nice of your mother to let me have these old sheets of hers, wasn't it?" he said. "One for me and one for the dummy downstairs."

"You mean my *mother* knew all about this?"

"Sure," Poetry said. "That's why she was so willing to let you and Wally come to sleep in my tent tonight."

"It's hard to believe," I said.

Poetry said, "Oh, I had to talk her into it. I ate a whole piece of blackberry pie while I was doing it."

A minute later Big Jim called the meeting to order. In another minute, as soon as we were quiet, he said in a very dignified voice, "This meeting is called in honor of Walford Sensenbrenner, who has been spending the week with us, helping us have a good time. It is in honor of Alexander the Coppersmith also, without whom we couldn't have had half as much fun. He's a great dog. Isn't that right, gang?"

"Right!" a chorus of different pitched voices said.

"And we want them both to come back again, don't we?"

"Right!" all of us, including Bill Collins, said.

I watched the mustache on Big Jim's face and wondered how long it would be before I could grow that much fuzz on my own upper lip and be able to make as nice a talk as he was making right that second.

"We like you, Walford," he went on, "and we think you are a great guy. Also, we want you to know we would like to make you an associate member of the Sugar Creek Gang, if you are interested. That's why this meeting was called tonight. All you have to do is to promise to read your Bible every day and pray every day and go to Sunday school and church every Sunday and try to live a clean, honest life."

Big Jim stopped, and you could feel question marks floating all around the dimly lit attic room. You could *see* a question mark on every one of the gang members' faces.

Everything was very quiet for a minute. Even Alexander the Coppersmith downstairs was quiet. I saw Wally's freckled face flush, and he swallowed hard a couple of times before he answered. "Y–y–yes, sir, I'd like to try."

Right away there was a feeling running up and down my spine that was better than being scared by any imaginary ghost.

"And now," Big Jim stated, "your membership token." He nodded to Little Jim, who reached out and took a small white package off the table where it had been lying beside the lantern and handed it to Big Jim.

"It's from all of us—from you, too, Bill. We kept the secret from you till tonight so it would be easier for you to keep it from Wally."

He handed the little white package to Wally, who gulped and said, "Thank you."

When Little Jim said, "Open it," he did. It was a beautiful little reddish brown leather New Testament like the kind all the gang owned and every one of us read every day of our lives.

Then Poetry, who was sitting beside his old-fashioned phonograph, all of a sudden turned it on. Right away there was music—a whole chorus of bird voices, beginning with the juicy notes of the kind of red-winged blackbird that sings in the bayou. A second later it was joined by a half-dozen other birds all singing at once.

That sounded like the house wren that has its nest in a little brown house on our clothesline post and the wood thrush that builds its nest in the papaw bushes not far from the Sugar Creek bridge and a dozen mockingbirds and canaries all at once, all sounding very happy. In the loft of the old toolshed, with seven boys' faces all lighted by the light of Poetry's lantern, it was a wonderful sound.

Then, almost before I knew what was happening, there was actual harp music and a violin and a marimba and a male quartet singing a song we sometimes sang on Sunday morning in the Sugar Creek church. It was a song called "Carry Your Bible with You." The chorus of it went:

> Take it wherever you go,
> Take it wherever you go.
> God's message of love,
> Sent down from above,
> Oh, take it wherever you go.

Some crazy tears got mixed up in my eyes just then, and for a minute I couldn't see very well. But I knew if I could have looked carefully in the dim lantern light, I'd have seen a few tears shining in the rest of the gang's eyes.

And that was that, and a very wonderful that at that. It was a surprise the way things had turned out. Poetry himself got a surprise, because he hadn't counted on Alexander's being tied to the tent pole and having the tent pulled down at midnight—or rather, at ten o'clock.

But then it was time for all of us to get some sleep because tomorrow was another day—Wally's last day and also his dog's last day.

As soon as we were downstairs and outdoors, I heard a car honking and lights were turned on in the lane.

"There's our taxi," Big Jim said, and he and Circus and Dragonfly and Little Jim started toward it.

"Who is it?" I asked.

The horn sounded like a car horn I'd heard before a few hundred times at our house, when Dad honked a friendly little honk from the plum tree to remind Mom that he was ready to go and please hurry up and get her nose powdered and her hat straight enough or crooked enough to go wherever she and Dad were going.

Even Dad had been in on Wally's initiation! I thought, as Wally and Alexander and Poetry and I went back to the tent to get some sleep.

Wally and Poetry walked on ahead, and Alexander and I and the tent pole followed. "Next time we take a walk," I said to Alexander, "it will be in the daytime."

13

I'd certainly hate to live at Poetry's house because, even if his parents would let him, a boy wouldn't have a chance to sleep as long as he wanted to in the morning. It seemed I hadn't any more than wound the alarm of my polecat clock again and set it for seven in the morning than about forty-seven squawky-voiced young roosters started to crow, telling us it was daylight. At the same time all the cows and calves started to bawl, and about twenty-five guinea hens began to sing or scream or squawk or whatever it is those scrawny-necked, topknot-headed, white-speckled, black-legged barnyard fowls do when they're happy.

I never saw a boy get up so cheerfully as Poetry did. He started to whistle the minute he was awake. When I tried to shush him, he said, "Can't a boy be happy if he wants to?"

"Who wants to?" I groaned and turned over to try to sleep again.

"You do," he said.

Just that minute his mother called from their back porch, "Yoo-hoo, Leslie," which is Poetry's real name, "you boys awake?"

And Poetry's voice went squawking back through the slanting canvas roof of the tent, saying, "Bill and Wally don't want any pancakes."

For some reason that made me wake up as fast as I had ever waked up in my life. I remembered the six hundred or more buckwheat cakes I had eaten at his house during my life.

I rolled over and up to a sitting position. Wally was still asleep. I looked toward his cot in the corner and at his red hair on the pillow, and it was almost like looking at myself lying there.

I started to call, "Wake up, you sleepyhead," but Poetry lifted his forefinger to his lips and jerked a thumb toward Wally, shaking his head at the same time.

I looked closer and noticed that Wally's right hand was clasping something while he slept, and it was the little New Testament the gang had given him last night. All of a sudden I got a happy thought. Every time I thought of it that day and all the rest of the summer, it made me glad Wally had come to our house. The thought was mixed up with Sylvia's dad's sermon and Robert Louis Stevenson, and it was: *The gang has given Wally a light he can carry around with him, and he can turn it on anytime he wants to.*

Just then Alexander started to help the crowing roosters and the singing hens and the clacking guineas outside, letting everybody know it was time for pancakes.

And so the day was started. It was a day that was to be better and also worse than any we had had yet.

I got a new idea while I was dragging myself

into my clothes. I might be making a big mistake to take Alexander over to Mr. Groenwald and confess what he had done—if he had done it. After all, Alexander was Wally's dog, and what right had one red-haired freckle-faced boy to confess the sins of another red-haired, freckle-faced boy's dog?

When I got outdoors into the sunshiny morning, I walked over to where Alexander was tied to the clothesline post. I noticed the utility can was lying on its side beside him. He came toward me with a friendly expression on his face, but instead of jumping up on me, he wagged his tail and smiled and crouched at my feet the way dogs do when they want you to like them and are a little bit afraid of you.

As I looked down at him, it seemed I couldn't stand the thought of his having to be shot, which would be the same as having the light of his life blown out like a boy blowing out a lantern. Nobody could ever light Alexander's light again, and they would bury his body under a swamp rosebush or somewhere in the woods or along the bayou, and he'd stay buried and wouldn't come up again like a grain of corn you plant in a cornfield. Never again would there be a pretty copper-colored dog playing innocently around in the woods or anywhere.

And it'd be all my fault, I thought.

It seemed a lot worse to have a boy's only dog die than for Mr. Groenwald to lose two lambs when he had a dozen others just like them.

So there I was, on the fence in my mind

again, not knowing what to do. Yesterday I had talked to God about it, and it seemed He had told me what to do. But today it seemed that if I confessed Alexander's sins to Mr. Groenwald, and Alexander had to be shot as some dogs in the Sugar Creek neighborhood had been, I'd be to blame for his death. The fifty dollars it might cost me seemed like nothing—I'd be willing to pay ten times that much if I had to in order to save his life.

I quickly dropped down on my knees on Alexander's cedar-treated mattress and hugged him, letting his cold nose touch my face. While I was there like that, I said, "Dear Father, please show me for sure what to do."

Then Wally and Poetry came storming out of the tent to start their day, and we all went into the house to eat pancakes. Wally gave Alexander his dog biscuits first, so that he would be through eating by the time we were.

While we were at the table, Poetry said, "I saw Mr. Groenwald drive past with his truck Saturday. He had a brand-new gate. I'll bet Old Man Paddler's orchard would be a nice safe place for our next gang meeting."

That gave Wally an idea. And that was the reason that, when he and I loaded our luggage into my red coaster wagon and started out toward the Collins house, we had our polecat utility can with us. We were going past the orchard on the way home to get as many apples as we could carry for Uncle Amos and my red aunt to take back with them to Memory City.

"Maybe Mother will give me two dollars for them, which is what you have to pay for a bag of nice big apples at the store there."

"Remember it's my can. I found it," Poetry said as we started off.

Alexander, with his long tongue hanging out, pulled Wally along on the other end of the leash. And the wagon, with its longer tongue, was being pulled by me.

In only a little while we reached the orchard, and, as Poetry had said, there was a brand-new gate. It wasn't hung yet, but was just standing against the old one and was fastened to it by baling wire. But the bull probably didn't know that.

It was a no-sag kind of gate, the kind Dad had at the other end of our barnyard. It had one strand of barbed wire at the bottom so pigs wouldn't enjoy crawling under it, and two at the top so cows and horses wouldn't put their necks over and mash it down. In between was strong wire netting.

We tied Alexander to the fence to guard the wagon for us and to keep him from running around in the pasture and stirring up the temper of the bull. The cattle were about one hundred yards away from the gate at the time.

In seconds Wally and I were over in the orchard helping ourselves to hatfuls of great big apples, which Old Man Paddler said the gang could have anytime we wanted them. We carried our hatfuls again and again to the fence and pushed them through into the wagon and the utility can.

Then all of a sudden I heard the sound of a motor. Somebody in a truck was driving through the pasture straight toward us. Alexander growled and strained at his leash and started barking. Wally yelled for him to stop. Even before I knew who it was, I felt sure it would be Mr. Groenwald. My heart started beating fiercely, and I was scared of what might happen.

A minute or so later, the truck was there and stopping by the gate, and it *was* Mr. Groenwald. "Hi, there, boys," he called cheerfully. "Saw you over here and thought now would be a good time to hang the gate. Want to help me a minute? It'll save me hiring somebody else, and you can make a quarter apiece."

Mr. Groenwald climbed out of the cab of his truck, and pretty soon we were all working on the gate. I had helped Dad hang quite a few gates in my life and had a few good ideas of my own, which I gave Mr. Groenwald at no extra charge.

"You boys keep on the watch for Old Red. He's been a little nervous lately, and I don't trust him. If he gets too close, just climb into the wagon box, and you'll be safe enough."

Pretty soon we had the old worn-out gate off. We were lifting the new one and trying to fit its hinges into the screw hooks on the gatepost when I heard a sound of hoofed feet running in our direction. Without even turning around, I knew that some four-footed danger was coming. When I did look and saw what it was, my heart leaped into my mouth, and I was scared stiff.

"Quick, you boys! Get into the truck!" Mr. Groenwald ordered. He whirled around, clasped Wally by the middle, and scooped him up and into the truck's wagon box as quick as a flash. As quick as another flash, I made a leap for the top of the top sideboard, and almost right away I was inside beside Wally, both of us having landed on a little pile of firewood.

In another minute, Mr. Groenwald would be safe, too. He dived for the truck's cab, maybe so he could start the motor and get us out of the way of Old Red's horns. The door he tried to open was on the steering wheel side, but somehow it had locked. He would have to rush around to the other side to get in, and that was the side the bull was coming from.

It was already too late because Old Red was within a few yards of him. Mr. Groenwald dashed around the truck with the bull right after him. Round and round they went, and Wally got scared and started shouting directions to him. I yelled, too, not being able to help it.

Then things *did* go bad. Old Red got between Mr. Groenwald and the truck, and there wasn't a chance in the world for him to get in. The bull was standing head down, snorting and pawing in Mr. Groenwald's direction, and I could tell that a second later he would charge. Things were happening so fast I couldn't think or see straight. And then they started happening even faster!

All our yelling was enough to make Alexander wild. He never could stand to see anybody get into any noisy excitement without wanting to get into it himself. Maybe he had been waiting all week for just one chance to show us what he could do with a bull in a real fight.

Anyway, Alexander started to run frantically, first one way and then the other, getting stopped every time by the end of his leash, yanking and pulling and backing up and trying to get the collar over his neck, as he had done a few other times during the week. But I knew the collar was in the tightest notch it could be in, and he wouldn't be able to get loose.

Just then the bull charged like a streak of red lightning.

But Mr. Groenwald was a smart man. He made what is called a "reverse turn" in a basketball game and was out of the way of the bull, which went past headfirst like a ton of dynamite. If either one of his horns had caught Mr. Groenwald, it would have ripped a hole clear through him.

He didn't even have a stick with which to protect himself—or a pitchfork, as a farmer often does have when he is out in a field where a bull is.

Then I got an idea. If we could distract the bull's attention, we might help save Mr. Groenwald's life. As it was now, he was safe only as long as he could dodge Old Red. So I quickly stooped down, saying to Wally at the same time, "Let's help. Let's wham the bull in the nose and side and everywhere with sticks of firewood!" And we started to throw them as straight as we could toward the bull without hitting Mr. Groenwald.

One of Wally's sticks hit Old Red *ker-whack* on the nose, which only made him madder than ever. And since Mr. Groenwald was the only one the bull could see, he let out a wild bellow of temper and started on another head-first dash straight for him, snorting and bellowing as he charged.

But then those sticks of firewood helped in a way I never would have dreamed they could. I don't know what went on in Alexander's mind, but when he saw those flying pieces of wood, he went absolutely crazy. It was his signal to go after them.

The next thing I knew, the fence post he was tied to was shaking like our corner grape-arbor post, and he was yanking and pulling backward as though he had gone mad. His breaking the leash right at the collar happened too fast for me to see it, but from what happened next, I knew he was free.

A copper-colored flash shot up toward the top of the fence and over it, as he had done with every other fence in the Sugar Creek neighborhood. The next second he was on our side, starting to do what he had wanted to do all week—show a big, fierce red bull that he wasn't any bigger or more dangerous to him than a giant snapping turtle had been.

It would have been one of the most entertaining fights I had ever seen if it hadn't been the most dangerous. Alexander shot like a copper arrow straight for Old Red. I never saw a dog run so fast. In seconds, his sharp teeth were nipping at the heels of the bull, and he was barking and yelping and dashing in and biting and jumping back. Then he grabbed Old Red's tail and held on.

The bull whirled around, taking Alexander with him as he turned and hurling him almost fifteen feet when Alexander's teeth let loose. Seeing his copper color and probably thinking it was red, Old Red started after him.

And that's how Mr. Groenwald got his chance to get to the cab and climb in it in time to be saved—and just in time. He slammed the door and started the motor, and the truck started to move.

"Wait for Alexander!" Wally screamed. "He'll be killed!"

But it all happened so fast that we didn't have to wait.

Alexander was out there diving all around the bull's lowered head, barking and getting out of the way so quick that the fierce monster didn't have a chance to hurt him. The only way he could possibly have hurt him would be to rush him when Alexander was too close to the fence or the gate.

Just then, Wally let out a terrified scream as

Alexander dashed in—not at Old Red's heels or tail but straight toward his lowered head, where he sank his teeth into the bull's nose and held on.

Old Red let out a fierce bellowing snort and, with the big bulging muscles of his neck, gave his head a quick toss. Alexander went up with it, getting a fierce, fast, free ride into the air. The bull shook him loose at the same time.

And when Alexander came down, he came down in the wagon box beside Wally and me—right where we wanted him—and his life was saved, too!

The bull, not seeing where Alexander had gone and not knowing what had become of him, stopped and stared and snorted at the truck, hearing the motor running and probably wondering, *What on earth?*

We gave Alexander a quick examination, and he didn't seem to be hurt a bit. So he wouldn't even have to have first aid when we got home, as he had to have after his battle with the mud turtle at the swamp. We did have to hold him in the wagon though, or he would have jumped out again. He wasn't satisfied with his fight. It had ended too soon.

Well, we got out of the pasture as easy as anything. Mr. Groenwald drove up alongside the woven-wire fence, on the other side of which were our wagon and apples, and all we had to do was climb down the other side, which we did. The bull, not seeming to be interested in a truck, started back toward his fifteen cows, probably to brag to them about how he had licked two boys and one man and a fierce copper-colored wild animal of some kind.

"I'll get Old Red penned up tonight when he comes into the barnyard," Mr. Groenwald said to us before he drove away. "By the way, that's a wonderful dog. He'd be a big help to a farmer. Want to sell him? I could train him to be a good stock dog. Maybe if I'd had him around last week, I wouldn't have had two of my lambs killed. There goes my dinner bell. The missus has dinner ready."

Before I could have said anything to him, even if I had decided to, it was too late. He raced his motor, and his truck moved on down the pasture toward his farmhouse on the other side. But one thing I knew for sure, and that was that Harm Groenwald would never want to have Alexander shot when he finally found out he had killed his two lambs—if he had. Anyway, I would have to wait until later to tell him what I knew.

14

It was two happy, red-haired, freckle-faced boys that pulled my little red wagon full of luggage and apples back to the lane we had left and on toward our house.

One thing Wally asked me just before we got to the lane was about his initiation last night. He said, "Is that the way to become a Christian—what they did to me last night?"

"No, no," I said. "That was just making you a member of the gang. Anybody who promises to go to Sunday school and church every Sunday and to read the Bible and pray every day can be a member."

"How do you get to be a Christian, then?"

Wally hadn't been to church very much in his life. I'd hardly realized that he might not even know how to become a Christian. So I told him what I had heard Sylvia's dad say many times in church. "Believe in the Lord Jesus, and you will be saved."

Then I had to explain it to Wally so he could understand. "It's just like riding on this wagon. Sylvia's dad would say, 'You just get in and ride and trust whatever is pulling you.' You believe in the Lord in your heart the same way."

"Who's Sylvia's dad?" Wally wanted to know, and I told him.

As we rambled along, neither one of us saying anything for a while, I could tell he was thinking about what I had told him. I decided that even if he wasn't a Christian yet, he would probably be one before long. Because if a boy read his Bible and prayed every day, the Lord Himself would turn on the light in his heart.

There was a shortcut to our house if we went through the edge of Big Jim's woods, so we decided to take it. Just as soon as we got to maybe within an eighth of a mile from home, I spotted a little black and white animal nosing around an old stump not far from a big rail pile. It was a skunk all by itself. It wasn't big enough to be the mother skunk that used to live under Poetry's toolshed. It was a smaller one, probably one of her kittens.

Boy oh boy, I hoped Wally, and especially Alexander, wouldn't see it—or that Alexander wouldn't smell it. He'd make a dive for it, and it wouldn't get away. Then we'd have the tail end of Wally's visit ruined completely!

But it was already too late. Alexander *had* noticed it, and he stopped and sniffed and started a gruff growl in his throat. He wasn't more than ten feet from me at the time, and our only hope to save us from a perfume shower bath would be to stop him quick, which I managed to do by saying, "Here, Alexander!"

I quickly picked up a stick and waved it, and he started toward me as he nearly always does until I've thrown the stick. Then he gallops after it.

Of course, I didn't throw it. Instead, when he got to within a few feet of me, I dove for his collar, caught it, and hung onto him for dear life.

Just then Wally saw the kitty. Well, that was just as bad. He wanted it, too, and the next thing I knew, he had swooped down onto our wagon, grabbed the utility can, dumped out the apples into the wagon and all over the ground, and grabbed the can's lid. Away he ran like a crazy boy, straight for that black and white woods kitty.

"Come back!" I yelled to him. "This is your last day! And your folks will be as mad as a hornet! You can't take a skunk home with you in your car, and you can't even go home yourself!"

My words on Wally's mind were like pouring water on an umbrella. He kept on running straight for the old stump the polecat was digging around. The kitty saw him and heard him at the same time, and I knew—*knew* what would happen. It had to happen.

Wally wouldn't know what to do when the kitty's tail shot up like the plume on Little Jim's mom's hat. I was holding on for dear life to Alexander's collar and also to his neck and trying to quiet him, and I knew he would have to break his collar to get away from me.

Then I got a surprise. Wally seemed to remember exactly how Circus had told him he had caught the skunk we had seen him catch quite a while ago. The very second the little woods cat saw Wally that close to him, he swished his tail straight up in the air and began dancing with his front feet, as much as to say, "I hate red-haired people! One move out of you and your name is mud."

And Wally didn't move a muscle. He just stood there with the utility can in one hand and both eyes glued to the skunk.

I crouched beside Alexander and cringed.

Alexander strained and growled, probably thinking, *What on earth? Just give me one chance to do what I've been wanting to do all week, and I'll go back to my city life a happy dog.*

Then the kitty decided he had been quiet long enough and that maybe Wally wasn't going to hurt him after all, so he lowered his flag and started off on a trot toward the rail pile, where I supposed his mother and the rest of her family had moved after they left Poetry's dad's toolshed.

Wally trotted beside that kitty—about eight feet from it—when all of a sudden, just as I had seen another kitty do when Circus had been trotting beside it, it stopped again and swished its flag straight up.

Wally went into action, except that he didn't do as well as Circus. He started toward it like a shot, but one of his feet stumbled over the other, and he landed in a sprawl beside the skunk. Reaching out, he made a grab for its tail and missed, and I knew it was too late. Too absolutely late. The last day of his week was ruined.

But Wally was no dumbbell. He grabbed

again while he was still on the ground, and there was some lightninglike action that I couldn't see, and the kitty disappeared inside the utility can. The lid was clamped on, and Wally was up and sitting on the can and grinning and yelling, "Come on! I've got him. I've got a skunk!"

And he had!

It was good news, but it was bad news too, I thought. Alexander the Coppersmith and I left the wagon and started over to where Wally was.

"He doesn't smell a bit!" Wally cried. "He didn't even get a chance to shoot!"

Well, I knew better than that. That skunk had had time to shoot at least three times before his back feet were whisked off the ground, and he probably had used the rest of his six shots after he got into the utility can, which we were supposed to use to put apples back in and take them home.

But then I did get a surprise. There *wasn't* any smell. There actually wasn't. *What on earth?* I thought.

Just then I heard somebody coming toward us. Looking up, I saw Circus himself coming on an excited run as fast as he could, yelling, "Hey, you guys! You seen anything of a skunk around here? My pet skunk got away, and I can't find it anywhere!"

And I remembered that Poetry had told me that the reason the mother skunk had moved her family was because Circus had caught another one of her kitties. And, of course, he had already had it "de-skunked" so it wouldn't smell.

It had been a wonderful week—simply wonderful. Boy oh boy. Wally had caught a skunk as he had wanted to, even if Circus had caught it first. Then I found out Circus had planned to give it to Wally as a pet, anyway. Also, Alexander had had his fight with the bull as he wanted to. And something else even more important than all that had happened to Wally's heart.

Later in the afternoon, when Uncle Amos and my red aunt and Wally drove away with Wally and Alexander the Coppersmith and his cedar-treated mattress in the back of the car and the black and white woods cat in the front in a dogproof cage, I watched the car going up the road.

And as the white dust moved out across Dad's cornfield, a little whirlwind started up in our barnyard. It was such a lively and friendly one that I left "Theodore Collins" on the mailbox near where I had been standing and started on the run across the barnyard after it, to toss myself into it as I liked to do.

As I ran, feeling sad and wonderful at the same time, a flock of old hens that had been dusting themselves not far from the iron pitcher pump came to life and scattered in every direction. Mixy, who had been nosing around the grape arbor, must have thought my fast-flying feet were Alexander the Coppersmith's, because she whirled around quick and started off like a black and white streak toward the barn.

I followed along in the spiraling little windstorm until it reached the edge of the cornfield and went whirling out into it, making the happy little noise I had read about once in a poem in Poetry's book:

> The husky, rusty rustle
> Of the tassels of the corn . . .

Even though I had to stop at the edge of the cornfield, my thoughts went sailing round and round in a little whirlwind of their own, flying higher and higher into one of the prettiest skies I ever saw.